RECKONING

Blue Blooded Brothers Book 5

Sofia Aves

RECKONING

Blue Blooded Brothers Book 5

Sofia Aves

First Edition
Published by Little Quail Press
Cover Art by JS Designs Cover Art
Editing Services provided by A. Strom - Edits with a Coffee Addict
www.redpensandcoffeebeans.wordpress.com/
www.facebook.com/redpensandcoffeebeans/

ISBN 978-1-922448-21-7

CONTENTS

BLUE BLOODED BROTHERS SERIES

COWBOYS & WESTERNS

PARANORMAL ROMANCE

<u>TRICKSTER'S LAW</u>
<u>A PORTRAIT IN ASH AND LACE</u>

VIII

DEDICATION

To my writing tribe -
thanks for helping me get here!

CHAPTER ONE

LIAM

Chatter filled the small area at the top of Micah's warehouse, his blue monster truck parked below us in its slightly battered state. Arms and legs tangled around fully clothed bodies in a pizza orgy worthy of Roman times.

Micah's mother had cooked.

That we were all in one place was a rare occurrence — but after the rough times and few wins the team had experienced recently, relaxing together was a blessing.

Selena stretched across me, snagging the last of the garlic bread as Cal's long-fingered paw swiped for it. Mutters began under her breath I knew would develop into the sort of blazing temper I adored. Dark curls bounced over Selena's shoulders as she jerked out of his reach just in time.

"Mine." A tiny growl purred between her lips.

I hid a smile as Selena's gaze slid to meet mine. Tucking her dark denim-clad legs beneath her, she gave me a saucy grin and snuggled on the other side of Mila's very pregnant belly, propping her elbow on the arm of the sofa.

I curled my arm around her denim encased calf and reached up to liberate the second to last piece of bread from her hands. My best friend might live with me, most of the time; I even got the liberty to kiss her on occasion. Less than I wanted, and less than she would have liked, I knew. But we balanced on the edge of a not-quite relationship, neither wanting to push too much or too far, so no one pushed at all.

After her last run-in with Logan's *messenger*, I'd finally managed to kiss her, which led to a key slipped into her handbag. But now, we were at an odd standoff where neither of us was prepared to risk the years of friendship in case either of us — *me* — fucked it up.

It made for a continual tease, and so I took out my energy in the smallest ways.

Selena let out the cutest squark that had me wanting to haul her over my shoulder and take her home. But as her hands clawed the air where I held the mouth-watering bread out of her reach, I knew I wouldn't take advantage of what she would offer, what she had always wanted. Hell— what *I* wanted.

Anything capitulating between us was long overdue.

"Liam, you give that back, or I'll lock you out of the house when we get home," she threatened, taking a swipe at me.

I stuffed the bread in my face and caught her hand, giving the back of it a garlic-y kiss. Selena pouted, her thick lashes brushing her cheeks.

The girl I'd never properly claimed, sexy as sin and gorgeous as hell.

Danny and Micah cheered from across the room. The two youngest members of my task force filled the sofa with the combined girth of a couple of elephants. Micah's mechanic and girlfriend, Jimmy, was squished between them, her tiny frame almost disappearing, except for a flash of bright green hair.

The boys let out their catcalls that echoed inside Micah's enormous warehouse.

"Take him down, Selena!"

"Here, catch," Danny called, flinging something across the room.

Every muscle in my body tensed at the movement. My heart beat too hard in an irregular staccato against my chest as my body flooded with adrenaline by long honed reflex. Inhaling deeply, slowly, I kept my face smooth, fighting the deep-seated need to cover her body with mine and take us both to the floor.

But there was no threat here.

That didn't prevent the urge to retch the layer of fine, stale dust that coated my tongue, though the desert was long behind me. I swished the garlic remains in my mouth to wash the sand away in a reflex swallow born of too many overseas tours.

Selena grabbed the pillow tossed in my direction with a sure arm and drew it back threateningly, aiming at me.

"Nah, he's a hard-arse. Doesn't need one." Danny winked at Selena.

I levelled him with a cool glare that was only half-truthful as Micah's warehouse replaced the desert. Fine, pink grains gave my vision a hazy-edged frame.

"It's my house, babe." I squeezed her leg gently with my other hand, trailing my fingers to circle them around her ankle, contemplating her threat to lock me out. "You won't."

A challenge sparkled in her eyes, though she shifted a little closer, heat emanating from her body across the small, charged patch of air between us.

Beside her, Mila yawned. "I need to get home," the pregnant woman said to the room at large, pressing a hand to Cal's knee.

He helped lift her from the lounge, a large diamond winking at me from her hand.

I squeezed Selena's undecorated fingers, running the pad of my thumb over her left ring finger. She entangled our hands, weaving her slim, elegant fingers through mine, wriggling her way off the sofa.

"I'll take you home," she said to Mila, looking over her shoulder to Cal and me. "You two come home before the sun rises. It's Monday tomorrow, and we have to get back into the—"

"Don't you dare say his name!" Cal half-yelped, tossing a balled paper serviette at her. She caught it and flung it back, smacking him in the forehead. Cal rubbed the spot mournfully. "You'll jinx us," he grumbled, kissing Mila. One hand curved around her bump in a protective measure I envied.

It's your own fault you don't have what he's got, you stupid bastard.

Opposite us, Black wrapped his arms around Jenny.

I drew my gaze around the room, catching movement where Micah's enormous frame pressed into a too-small space beside Danny, Laura curled at his legs. Jimmy's mermaid green hair dangled from the edge of the sofa, where she hung upside down from Micah's lap.

The whole team in one place.

My family.

Everyone was safe and happy, for once. I shook my head at the strangeness of it; I couldn't remember the last time we were all this way. With Logan's case heading to trial, and a sympathetic judge, we were finally free of the madman.

"Eight years," I murmured, letting Selena pull me up.

Eight years of hell, wondering who he would attack next. And how.

"What?" she asked me with a playful frown, tracing along my hairline with a delicate touch that made me want to crush her against me. There were more greys there than dark hairs, now. "Are you okay?"

"I'm fine." I gave into the urge and pulled her to me, kissing her a touch too hard. Selena drew back with a gasp, her cheeks flushing a soft pink. Wide eyes held mine, sending a double shot of arousal straight to my cock. "God, you're beautiful."

She mumbled something unintelligible against my chest, snuggling into me. Her fingers curled into my shirt, stroking at my scars beneath in her own little possessive gesture.

I want to take you home and do everything I've ever wished to do to you.

But I knew I wouldn't. Instead, I held on tight when she wriggled in my arms, not caring if the entire room was a witness to our PDA.

Cal caught my eye over her shoulder from the recliner next to us. He nodded, jerking his head toward the stairs.

"I'll see you soon. Don't wait up for me," I murmured into the wild tangle of waves and curls that covered her lithe frame.

Selena's mouth opened, her eyes narrowing as she took in my tone. "You know I'll be working."

I tucked a dark, glossy lock behind her ear. "You should sleep."

"Mmm," she kissed me again, untangling her fingers from mine with a reluctance that made my heart thump harder in the cage of my chest.

I am so blessed with this woman.

Cal muttered something about getting a room. Selena broke away from me, the high flush in her cheeks matching bright eyes that she hid beneath thick lashes.

Mila rolled her eyes, waddling over to kiss Cal on the cheek.

"I really do need to go home," she yawned. "Thanks, Micah. For hosting."

The huge man rose and engulfed her, kissing the top of her head. He murmured something in her ear. She smiled up at the giant, laughing at whatever he had said.

Shouts called out as she descended the stairs, waving off the boys' help but allowing Cal to escort her.

Laura snuggled on Danny's lap while she argued the finer points of car racing with Micah. Jimmy piped up, adding her voice as Micah picked her up, settling her in the middle of the sofa framed by the two enormous men.

My family.

Selena's lips brushed against mine one last time. She followed Cal and Mila down the stairs, slightly hunched as she watched over her pregnant friend, hands extended.

I stood in the centre of the room, the small space now empty without her in it. Heading across to Micah's kitchenette from his lounge area, I grabbed a fresh beer from the fridge, turning to lean my back on the cool bench top.

Without a case to work, tomorrow would be somewhat different. The team had been on a hiatus for too long, working smaller cases. Once Logan had been denied bail, his case should have been out of our hands. Instead, the psychotic bastard had integrated himself into every aspect of our lives. Selena had finally found a judge to handle Logan's trial — the first two had been dirty — and now we had a court date.

There'd already been talk of dissolving the task force now Wayde Logan's manhunt had finally reached its conclusion. And even if the room wasn't full of men — and women — who had become more than workmates during our trials together, it seemed a waste to disband them and throw them out into individual careers. I had no doubt that every one of the boys would fly to heights on their own, but as always, we were stronger together.

I dragged a hand through my short hair, though it still felt long to me, fifteen years after I'd left the army. Three years as a special ops sniper had formed a hard man who hid in the suit of a softer one driving a desk.

Selena was still wading through the mess of my head, though my patience with therapy was lesser these days.

"Feels odd, huh?" Cal appeared by my side, jerking me out of memory lane. I sipped my beer to avoid answering. "What do we do tomorrow morning?"

"Find a new job?" I snorted, only half-joking.

"Might need to. How long's it been?"

"Man, of us all, you're the one with a running calendar in his head."

Cal grinned. "Yeah, well. My fuck up in the first place, letting Logan escape."

"Are you seriously still blaming yourself for that?" I stared straight ahead, over the railing into empty space. "Hell, that was a long time ago."

The image of Cal's first truck busting open the bank front where Mila had worked burned before my eyes, though I had only ever been told the story. It had become something of a local legend, earning Callum Dane his nickname of the *Great Dane.*

Cal was right, though. If we'd managed to catch Logan at the first opportunity, we would all be in different places right now.

"Should have all been over eight dammed years ago."

"I knew you were counting."

Cal rolled his eyes. "Did you ever doubt it? Seriously, Liam. You've saved my ass too many times over the years. I wouldn't have a career without the time you took mentoring me. Or Mila."

"Don't get all emotional on me. I might get honest with you," I warned, hiding my grin behind my beer.

"I've never seen you lie."

"That you know about," I countered.

"True." Cal yawned, wandering across the small space to settle back into the recliner he had occupied before. "You alright, there?" He spoke to Black.

Theo Black nodded to Cal over Jenny's head as she sank into his shoulder, spreading his hands to his ex-partner in a "why are you fucking with my peace?" gesture. The dark-haired man looked like he should be in a motorcycle clubhouse, not an integral part of a police task force.

I grinned when he looked away, running his fingers through Jenny's hair. Jenny, the foster mother of Logan Wayde's daughter. The one he left at the scene of the bank Cal had driven his car through.

In our own way, each of us was connected with Wayde Logan to some twisted degree, how he had affected our lives.

I'd lived Logan's case for eight bloody long years, and the details still niggled at me. We all had. His brother's flip — I groomed him to it during their incarceration period waiting on trial — had finally yielded enough to warrant having Joey released. But even though I had claimed him as part of the team, I knew that no one else really saw him that way.

Hell, I didn't see him that way.

But the scarred boy had his own life, now, providing he testified against his brother, and he wasn't under my eye all the time. Micah had taken that mantle onto his overly broad shoulders.

Cal's phone vibrated across the bench top. I gave it a small push, and Cal caught it without looking up.

"Fuck. It's Mandy," Cal groaned, snapping his head back on the lounge as he tossed his phone back across the counter. I caught it before it toppled off the edge. It vibrated again.

"She's not giving up, man." I grinned.

Poor bastard.

Danny looked over at us with a wry grin, his arm around Laura's shoulders. The young cop I could see as Cal's replacement one day when my task force lead filled my shoes — in the not so distant future if all went to plan — rolled his eyes. Danny had taken his fair share of Mandy's bullshit and backstabbing to the point it had almost screwed up his career. Still, the youngest member of the task force had come back stronger than ever.

If politics broke up the team Cal and I had worked so hard to bring together as a family, I'd be pissed.

Maybe pissed enough to retire and see if a certain dark-haired solicitor would consider an old grunt as a permanent partner.

Cal flipped his phone over, ignoring the constant buzzing. His ex had been on his tail since he'd first met Mila. Seeing as Cal was the king of obsession — his own with

Logan well known within our tight-knit group — maybe it was karma, though I wished Cal & Mila the freedom to live their own lives.

Across from them, Jenny curled into Black, still tentative with him in public. Logan had touched every one of us somehow; each of us bore his scars, some more visible than others.

A pang struck me, wishing Selena was still here, too. She usually wore long-sleeved tops to hide the thin, white line that marred her perfect skin from wrist to shoulder and had damn near ended her life.

I'd pulled the trigger in a situation for the first time in fifteen years, but it hadn't cost me a thing. All the gears still worked, and I was as numb and dead inside as ever. Selena had no idea — I'd never fully explained the lack of emotion I felt for each kill, though I knew she suspected whichever truth she believed. Over the years, I'd played along with each group therapy she'd dragged me to, pretending it had an effect.

Those were the easier scars to hide.

I missed her already. Tracing the outline of my keys in my pocket, I wondered when I could leave without being rude. My bed was colder every night she spent in my guest room.

Perhaps it was time to fill it with something greater than my shattered ego.

I let my gaze rest on every member of Cal's team — *my team* — that we had put together after Logan's first escape. Every one of them was exceptional in many ways. Comfortable within themselves as well as together, they made a formidable wall of intelligence.

It would be more than a waste to break them up, and I resolved to battle for their continued existence together as soon as I got into the office tomorrow morning — which wasn't too far off. I sighed, covering my yawn.

Danny leaned down to kiss Laura, where she curled at his feet, saying something none of us could hear, though her cheeks flamed as she laughed softly, her gaze holding his.

I looked away, not wanting to intrude on their own private moment. My heart ached for Selena, though we had nothing like what the rest of the team did. Not yet.

Maybe it *was* time to pull my head out of the sand and try to be worthy enough to have her in my life as more than just a bystander.

Selena had been my best friend for nearly two decades, and the terror that whatever shadow of a tentative relationship we had might dissolve when we took it further drove me to push her away. But the time for that grace period to end was coming, and we both knew it.

It just depended on which direction she wanted to take.

Cal straightened in the armchair, rubbing the back of his neck, and gave me the perfect excuse.

Chickening out, I jerked my head to the fridge. "Want another beer?"

He nodded, the deep circles beneath his eyes more evident without Mila by his side.

I grabbed at the fridge door as Cal's phone buzzed again. The thing vibrated across the smooth surface. I flipped by reflex as the message flashed on the screen.

Mandy.

I groaned in sympathy for Cal, my curiosity getting the better of me as I leaned over to see what tack she was taking now. Four letters in caps filled the white text box.

BOOM.

I had just enough time to take a snapshot glance at my family before it erupted in a haze of smoke and flame.

CHAPTER TWO

LIAM

My world narrowed to a cloud of dust, slants of street lights pouring into Micah's warehouse, where it lay cracked open, its innards tumbling out into the night air. Faint pings and thunks pummeled the ground and my skin, showering a muted haze of cement and brick.

Grit blasted my skin, graduating from grey to pink, the all-consuming warmth of the desert permeating my camouflage pants.

My knees were reduced to tenderised flesh against the desert floor. I crouched, frozen, blinking into the face of my spotter. A ragged hole half the width of his tactical vest sat where his torso should have been.

Thudding in my ears increased with the tempo of my heart as I reached towards the man who had been my friend, my partner, through too many tours. Numb hands travelled along his shoulders, but when I reached his face, it was Cal's.

Staring, I touched his cheek, the street lights slanting once again into the broken warehouse. I had zero control when my gaze ripped to Cal's chest, but it was whole. His shirt hung tattered to one side, blood swirling in a slurry of dirt beneath his inert frame. A block of concrete lay across his lower half.

Echoes of voices that might have belonged to another time reverberated dully around my head. Disconnected footsteps circled us, voices yelling in a language I didn't understand, the two moments blurring my reality in a combined fog of war.

I blinked around at the rubble surrounding us, peering through the dust as it returned to grey and the light darkened to the night of the industrial estate Micah lived in. The hollow rang in a muted whistle that wasn't really noticeable but was all-encompassing at once. My bruised brain fought through the sludge to focus on *now*.

Not something I would have thought I would ever have to experience again.

Rubble covered everything. What had been an entire warehouse — *a home* — now lay in deconstructed clumps of concrete and pipes. On the far side of the block, a crumpled metal heap leaned against the remaining wall, flaking blue paint into the haze. A headlight dangled sadly, sponsorship logos brushing against a twisted metal lump that might have once been a refrigerator.

A soft moan brought my focus to the body beneath me, but it hadn't come from him. Pressing two fingers to Cal's neck, I looked around, counting the weak flutter there in my head. It was slow — slowing — and I couldn't see anyone else.

Green flickered in my peripheral vision.

Jimmy squiggled out from beneath the remains of the balcony, coated in a liberal mat of concrete dust. She coughed, retching, and for an eternity, or a single moment, I abandoned the best friend I'd had for too many years to count.

Somewhere in the back of my head, I thanked an unknown deity that Selena and Mila had left the building before it had blown up. The rational part of my mind cared.

But in the darkest recesses, shut away for too long, a cold rage brewed.

I shut it away for just a little longer, closing the door on what I knew I was capable of, and focussed on everyone else before I lost my mind to selfish desires.

"Jimmy," I rasped, inhaling a puff of debris that should never enter a human's lungs. "Here," I stretched one arm across the cement block that lay across Cal's lower body, drawing the tiny woman up.

She thrashed, slapping at my arms in silent fury.

Opening my fingers, I let her drop and watched as she fell to her knees, pawing at the rubble in a frantic motion. A shoe emerged, then a smooth, hairless leg. The tan was visible even under the ash of his home.

I launched myself over her, hefting away a slab of concrete as though it were nothing. It crashed behind me, louder than before. Nodding to myself, I let my brain turn on as the automatic triage response returned in full force, trained into me despite the decades it had been out of use. The ringing between my ears quietened by a small degree. God knew how deaf we would all be after this.

I caught the laugh before it left my throat.

If we all lived.

Rage burned away the tears that came nowhere near threatening, turning them to vitriol and tucking them into the depths of my soul for use at some later date.

"Micah." Jimmy had no reservations as she hauled the big man up with her will alone. He wrapped a great paw around her tiny frame, lifting her with him in an engulfing hug before he set her down, his lips pressed to the top of her head.

I nodded to my feet. Micah fell to his knees, hefting the concrete away.

The bottom half of Cal's leg was coated in blood, dust and grit congealing in a scarlet stain over his lower half.

My mind told me there was little chance he would survive while my ears picked out the sirens wailing their way through the city streets. It was enough to jar me out of my stupor. If we could keep him from bleeding out before they arrived...I tore my shirt over my head, buttons pinging across the mess we stood in. I slashed my arms in opposite directions, tearing the material into several pieces and wrapped the strips around Cal's lower leg in the best field tourniquet I could manage.

Micah hovered at my shoulder.

"Find Black. Danny," I snapped, not looking his way. "Laura."

I didn't bother looking up; I knew he would do what was necessary without supervision. These guys were the best — they'd trained, worked their arses off to catch the asshole who'd just blown their lives apart.

Not one inch of me doubted this was Logan.

And every inch of me trusted my team.

I won't lose them again.

A shout from somewhere behind me paired with gargled chatter reached my still-deafened ears. The boys yelled to each other, but neither sounded as panicked as my head was, and that was a good thing. I couldn't deal with any more tragedy when I couldn't chase after the man who haunted every one of us.

Like everyone else who encountered or worshipped Logan, Mandy was just another pawn in the chaotic game he used to ruin lives.

I finished with Cal's leg as ambulances halted where the curb used to be. Debris tumbled out into the street. My mind left Cal as I transferred him into the paramedic's hands, explaining the situation to the local cops like an automaton.

I took it in a state of grace that I didn't have to explain who I was.

By the time I had told my story to three increasing superiors, my mind was distant, assessing from above the scene. While the uniforms chattered about, mice scavenging for clues on a rubbish heap when there weren't any to be found, I retreated from the noise. The clutter became nothing more than what my brain needed right now: a drone flying high, seeing everything around me as my fingers tapped frantically at my cracked phone.

My mind was a machine, and I knew better than to disrupt it before it gave me everything I needed to move forward.

I took in the information that Logan had escaped from listening to a phone call somewhere behind me. My fingers stopped tapping the screen, and I hit *call* instead.

"Liam!" Selena screeched in my ear.

"He's out." My words came out flat. Emotionless.

"Marcus called. I know. I have Mila. Where do you want me to go?"

"He blew up Micah's house."

"Oh, my god! Are you okay? Are you hurt! Who's hurt?" fear tore the words from her throat in a hoarse shriek.

I ignored the stress in her voice. Where did I want them to go? Hell, where was safe from this madman? He'd already had a man inside Selena's townhouse once before; there was a bloody good chance he could be inside *any* house I named. Or any vehicle.

My head ran with possibilities, my mouth working before my brain had finished, which was always dangerous.

"Your best friend. Where does she live?"

"You're my best friend, you big lug."

"Ah. Fine. Friends– find their mother's place, ah– no. Mila is in a tremendous amount of danger. You too, but—"

"Cal's baby. Yes," a cold note edged into her clear voice. "He would, wouldn't he? After all the years that Cal has ostensibly *taken* his daughter, he would be after Cal's family. His little corner of revenge. So, who? Where, Liam? How do we make them safe?"

How do I make you safe?

My stomach lurched at the betrayal I was about to utter. The thought of sending her to another man, even if he was her business partner in the law firm she owned, still stung me, but her safety was paramount. "Marcus. I'll send a detail to escort you plus one for the house."

There was silence on the other end.

"Selena?"

"I heard you." Her voice was muffled, rough. She sniffed softly, but I still heard it.

Shit.

"You can do this."

"Liam. Who—"

"No. Don't ask." *I can't answer.* Fear clutched at my chest as, for a single second, I stopped. My brain cleared as the solution presented itself; despite that, I hated the only choice Logan had left me. "Get to Marcus. Now. And... Keep the phone on charge... Mila—"

"Cal," her voice was so soft, I barely heard it.

"Marcus. Go," I said firmly. "Be safe, please. I can't—"

"I know. I will."

The words I couldn't say — had never said — lodged in my throat. I ended the call. Heedless of the fear rolling in my chest, I tamped it down before it exited my mouth in an inhuman roar. The ambulance doors closed with a snap, and I turned, ready to sprint after Cal.

A hand gripped my shoulder.

Laura, covered in grit and smiling, squeezed hard.

The haze of pink returned in a swath of stale dirt that coated my tongue. I shunted the memory away; there was a time and a place to wallow in failure, but this wasn't it.

"Micah's with him. Black didn't seem to realise he had a chunk of flesh hanging off his back, so he's being tended to... under the greatest duress. The paramedics can handle him. Well, sort of. Danny is there, too. Won't leave him alone. Is Mila coming?" She smiled brightly, though the bite of her teeth as they clacked together echoed in the haze.

My mouth opened to say *I don't give a shit who's got him* and closed it with a snap. Laura didn't deserve my rage. Only one man had earned that.

I can't ask her to see this. Mila. She'll lose the baby.

It wasn't until Laura dug her nails in that I realised I'd spoken aloud.

"It'll be okay, Liam." Jimmy's tiny fingers, almost child-like, gripped my other hand. "We can follow them. My car is over there."

Laura shot me a look. "Do you need to be here?"

I looked around at the uniforms stepping on every inch of evidence, and promised myself I'd run a crime scene etiquette forum once this was all over.

If I hadn't been arrested.

Or killed.

Flicking off a quick message to Joey, I let the girls tow me to Jimmy's white, rusty bubble of a car. The image of the tanned bodybuilder stuffing himself inside pulled me out of the darkness. I stared at the vehicle, appalled.

"Has Micah seen this? Does he fit in it? Has he *fixed* it?"

"Yes."

Both girls giggled, though Laura's skin tinged green. She pressed a hand to her mouth, tears flooding her eyes.

"It's okay," I squeezed her arm as she leaned forward, pressing her other hand to her stomach, "There's nothing wrong with laughing. It's okay to feel human, Laura."

Her head went down, and I knew she didn't believe me.

I didn't believe me.

Jimmy glanced quickly at me. Her experience before she had met Micah spoke volumes in her ability to focus and move forward, speaking as though we had never broken conversation. "...and, no. Sorta. I've made Micah drive it once. After-" s he broke off.

She didn't need to talk me through it; I was just as familiar with her recent trauma in our office as everyone else.

Yet another touch of Logan.

He was the acid that burned each of us, eating away at the strong exterior until we fell apart from the inside out. Now the best of us lay on a gurney, bleeding out.

It was a miracle Cal was the only one so badly injured.

Jimmy shifted, hopping on one foot and wiggling it. I studied her; if she had any hidden injuries, she was unlikely to tell anyone about them. Promising myself I would have someone look both girls over at the hospital, I nodded.

"I'll fit."

Laura cracked a wan half-smile, but Jimmy sped around her small car and slipped into the driver's seat.

I wasn't sure what was worse — the hour of not knowing if I would get to say goodbye to a man I considered my brother or the hour of Jimmy's driving.

Street lights morphed into lit skyscrapers as she drove through Melbourne's centre. No one spoke, all of us lost in our own heads.

The emergency ward had little space for parking when Jimmy pulled up. She skittered out of her seat to free me from the back of her bubble.

"Get in there. Go," she urged, sliding back into the driver's seat. "I'll find you."

No doubt she would.

I brushed a hand over my chin, noting that Micah had done well to maintain her affection after all that had happened between them.

"Let's go." Laura dragged me inside, negotiating with nurses and doctors, leaving me wondering if I could actually function on my own.

When we reached Cal's bed to find Mila hunched over him, I froze.

Her face lined with worry years before her time, she draped her rounded body over his bloodstained sheets. A pair of young nurses attempted to change them without dislodging her, mumbling gently to each other over the cacophony the emergency room had become. One triage nurse hooked IV lines and tubes in a tangle around the bed from various angles, other monitors beeping in a regular rhythm.

Cal was attached to more machines than I had ever seen attached to a living person.

My gut sank to somewhere around the height of my knees. I looked for something to hold on to that wasn't connected to my friend, his easy laugh rolling around in my head.

Usually, when there was this much mess, the heart had already given up.

I grabbed a nearby nurse.

"Should she be here?" I growled roughly, nodding to Mila, her tears puddling on her husband's sheets.

The nurse stilled, searching my face. "This area is for family, and...we need the police to be here to give you the answers." She disengaged my fingers while I laughed, but there was nothing humorous in it.

"We are the damned police." The words ripped from my mouth in a harsh sound, but I didn't care about niceties enough to wince.

And there aren't any answers coming. Not yet.

I let her walk away, unable to voice the words that still seemed so unreal.

Beeps assailed my ears. I stared as a medical team congregated around Cal's bed, more a flock of hens pecking their patient than anything else. Danny tugged Mila away with a gentleness I lacked, talking over her cries and desperation as they wheeled Cal away. His easy voice reached me over the muddle of voices, and while some rational part of me envied his calm in a crisis, a cold pool of fury began to flood my system.

Mila tugged from Danny's hands, the big man's face stretched tight, and I knew he had let her go. An air of helplessness surrounded us all as Black positioned himself in front of Mila, blocking her vision and her advance.

Two nurses exchanged glances as they approached the pair. I braced, prepared to dive in if they manhandled Mila, every nerve end firing though I held my position away from them. Black caught my eye with a tiny shake of his head. Breath whooshed from my lips, my hands flexing at my sides.

The nurses ignored Mila clawing at his chest, tearing at him, but the older man who had been her carer for five years, who thought of her as a sister, stood firm and took the brunt of her pain.

"It's okay." I couldn't tell if he mouthed the words or said them or who the lie was aimed at. Mila nodded into his chest, letting his arms surround her — the big brother who had cared for her through so much.

My own hands ached, wanting to be wrapped in a sea of waves, to find coffee for her, but my focus couldn't be on my own needs. I tracked Cal's progress through a set of doors, memorising which nurses attended him for future reference.

Black flinched in my peripherals as a nurse pressed her hands to his shoulder, patting him and clucking away what though she stood at least a head shorter than him. Another attempted to bandage him up, cleaning a large, open wound that mercifully seemed to have stopped bleeding. They tacked the skin back beneath a swath of white; his angel wing tattoo returned to its place.

All of us would bear scars from tonight. It was just that some were more visible than others.

Cold tickled my fingers. I looked down dispassionately as a tiny, grey-haired nurse yapped at me merrily, explaining the meaning of life to me while I stared at her, unhearing. She bandaged a long stripe on my arm that I hadn't noticed, passing me an ice pack that she gestured toward my face to use. I switched it to my other hand and placed it on a bubbler stand beside me, focussed on the controlled chaos before me.

The pain Logan had brought upon us.

I turned away. If Mila was here, then Selena was, too. Somewhere.

I found her loitering beside the coffee machine over the heads of rushing medical personnel dressed in an assorted array of medical garb.

"You should have gone to Marcus's house." I wrapped my arms around her, too tight. Her body pressed against mine, warming places that had turned numb. "I should be angry with you, but..." I pressed a kiss beneath her ear, inhaling her scent. The rage in me evaporated my tears before they reached the surface.

Selena's presence alone kept the darkness inside me from seeping out. "Cal—" she whispered, burying her head in my chest.

Her skin dimpled beneath my fierce grip, but she didn't protest, just stared up at me.

"He'll be okay." I held her gaze, willing her to believe my words.

Willing myself to believe them.

Beside us, Micah leaned against the wall, a girl tucked under each arm. Laura and Jimmy huddled against him, the boulder we all leaned on at some point or other. The challenge was not to break against him. He caught my eye as I studied them, swivelling to the place I'd last seen the nurses congregating, and I realised someone was missing, and I couldn't see her anymore.

"Where's Mila?" The familiar taste of panic rose into my mouth

"With Black."

I frowned, recalling the nurse attempting to fix him, his stoic facade as he tolerated their fuss. "How's Black?"

Micah's lips split in a grin. "Whining like a bitch. Mila is holding one hand. Danny's on Black's other side to hold him down because he won't take anesthetic and he won't sit still. But the tiny man nearly fainted at the sight of blood." He raised his eyes heavenward.

If Danny was anything, he wasn't small. But compared to the mountain of a man that was Micah, I supposed everything seemed tiny and delicate.

A giggle escaped at my chest level. Tangling my fingers in Selena's mussed hair, I tugged her closer to me and grinned ruefully. "Sounds about right."

A nurse bent to speak to Mila as another brought her back in, pushing a wheelchair the pregnant woman refused to use. Black trailed the entourage, a faint grin on his face as Mila sassed the nurse, sparkling with defiance.

Selena gently extracted herself from my hold and wandered over, tucking her hand beneath Mila's arm. She chatted easily, deflecting the barrage of questions aimed at her. After a minute, she waved me over.

"We're not supposed to stay, but she's allowing us to remain as support for Mila. There's a waiting room, and we can hang out there until Cal's surgery is finished." Selena's words snapped off, brittle. She pressed white lips together.

"Okay. We all go." I let her lead us to the area the nurse had mentioned, catching Danny and Black, but I didn't need to say anything; they both knew none of us could go home yet.

One by one, we settled in and waited.

CHAPTER THREE

SELENA

I pressed my back to the sterile wall of the waiting area just outside the room Cal had been wheeled into hours earlier. After spending hours being poked and prodded and constantly reassuring the nurses that the dust covering me came from a certain brooding male, and that I hadn't been at the incident, the measured silence was a twisted relief.

Momentarily.

The jarringly cold sensation of each new patch of painted concrete that seeped through my top was all that kept me awake. That, and everything running about in my head.

The urge to hit my phone, to call Marcus, to get Mila home and resting, to do *something* covered the ongoing mess inside my head with a flight reaction. Anything at all to maintain a busy front in the face of silence that had been comforting for a whole second. Chaotic action. My reliable fallback when things went to shit.

But I couldn't bring myself to leave Liam, where he stood, his spine perfectly straight, his shoulders in a tight line. The stance he returned to when the world around him dissolved.

Only a few years in the army was enough to break old habits to reprogram him into the machine that dealt with panic in such a simple manner.

Not all of us had that luxury.

I hadn't envied Liam until that moment. After years of hauling him from group therapy to couples therapy and eventually to the footpath where he could beat his demons into submission by putting them through their paces, he had managed the pretence that all was well. His lie had become who he was, and we had lived with it. Until now, and Logan.

His name burnt my tongue with bitters. We had spent so long on his case, Liam and Cal and the boys, Marcus and I at work. So many hours, so many run-ins, and just as we thought it was over...

I closed my eyes, running my fingers along my scar. My personal reminder of Logan's reach, how integrated into our lives he had become, and now he started anew. The thought of him free to terrorise any of us gripped me, and the bitters turned to bile as I tried not to stare at Mila.

But I wasn't alone in my panic-induced stasis.

Eight other people populated the space around Cal's hospital room door, waiting. It wasn't everyone's strength, but the boys handled it well, considering they, too, never stopped in their work. In their line of duty.

Liam stood opposite the closed door of Cal's room. He hadn't moved in over an hour. Neither fatigue nor distress showed on his face or in his stance. The training that was drummed into him back when had kicked in with full force.

The boys had long since fallen silent. Danny cradled Laura to his chest, where I was sure the tall, blonde woman had fallen asleep. Jenny and Jimmy chatted softly at the feet of the two big men who stood sentinel on the other side of Liam.

I knew Liam had to play the part, to be the example. No one was a robot, though he certainly tried — and often, succeeded. The boys needed to see the human side of him just as much as the impenetrable, badass aspect the stubborn man I loved seemed intent on portraying.

"You can let them see you're hurting. It's okay to be human, Liam." I tilted my head sideways, pressing my cold cheek to the wall that probably had a thousand fleeing germs scuttling across its sterile, overmedicated surface, but I didn't care.

Liam didn't move. He didn't speak. The only indication he gave that he heard me was the slightest flicker of his eyes beneath the prematurely lined face of a man who had seen a lifetime of pain before his time.

Paired with the salt and pepper of his hair, though he wasn't yet forty, it gave him a distinguished look I had always loved, though I cursed the pain that haunted him. His silver fox look, he called it. But those eyes did flicker, though his gaze never left Cal's door.

I sighed. "Fine. Be a hardass, you stubborn bastard."

The lines around his eyes crinkled. "I'm all of those things," he agreed softly, his shoulders shifting the slightest amount.

"Wait, did you just smile?" I peered at him, and the lines that had shifted in his face moved a smidge more.

"I'm not the only stubborn hardass here," he said, soft enough that no one else would hear him.

"At least there's a good reason I stay around, then." I slipped my hand into his, where they were tucked behind his back in an iron grip. Peeling one finger back after the other, wiggled my fingers into his open hand before they snapped closed around mine, imprisoning them there.

"How are you—" I cut myself off, not bothering to finish.

Liam wouldn't answer my questions about how he felt, not in the company of others, and not later, in the comfort and security of his home.

But he would do the utmost to protect his team, though not having Cal at his side would cripple the team. He would do it all, anyway, while the rest of us restrained our grief just enough to get by each day, wondering where the next attack would come from. But Liam would be the rock we all broke ourselves on, trying to measure up to him.

Liam had always been that way. Give, give, and give more until there was nothing left, and then he would crash.

He had stumbled over me at the end of my first semester at university when everyone was cursing their overly ambitious choices after orientation week and paying the penalty for it for the three-week exam block.

By then, he had already completed several deployments in Afghanistan. After that critical last tour, when he had come home alone, he had been asked to retire his commission in lieu of pursuing a high-level career. The senior ranks farewelled him with honours and a medal he had never looked at.

And that's how he found me: dark-eyed, frayed temper and bearing the shaking hands of caffeine-fueled students during the first exam block.

My hands had actually stopped trembling enough for my writing to be partially legible. I scrawled notes and case references that my first-year law courses required to be called up on demand, my head filled with a thousand new terms and definitions. I'd wrapped my hand around my giant coffee cup, only to find the thing was empty.

Grumbling, I pushed back my chair and rose — straight into Liam.

With reflexes born of too many years of training and a haircut that was still too fresh to be anything but military, Liam scooped his own drinks into one hand, cursing softly as he slopped dark ambrosia. His other hand wound around my waist, pulling me into him.

Dark eyes stared down at me, the laughter in them barely hiding the shadows that lurked there, and I was instantly intrigued.

At least, that's what I told myself as he called out for another coffee to replace the one he slopped, then presented both to me in a double stack.

"Why am I taking coffee from a strange man?" I asked, pressing my lips together to prevent the smile that wanted to creep across my face.

"Because you look like you need them," he nodded to where I had covered my small table in notes. "I've seen you in the lecture hall, sucking down those doubles like a thirsty camel."

"What a delightful image. Are you stalking me?" I *did* smile this time, nudging his side with my elbow, "creeper."

"Only enough to know you need both." He grinned back, the smile hiding the shadows, replacing them with a flirtatious young man who was otherwise too serious and far too handsome for his own good. "Liam McNamara." He took the two fingers I offered around the cups as I introduced myself.

Trying not to be caught staring, I looked down at my notes and couldn't remember what I had been looking for. I sighed. "I don't even remember what I was doing."

"See, you did need it." Liam began gathering my notes, stacking them out of sequence.

I swallowed back a squark of horror. "Ah, what are you doing?"

"Taking you up to the library. You've got nowhere near enough room here."

"I don't come here for the table space," I wiggled the coffees at him, still clutching the ones he had given me. "And aren't you getting one for yourself?"

Liam finished stacking my notes in a haphazard pile, sliding them into my bag and hooking it over his shoulder. His breath brushed my cheek as he leaned close for a long moment, and the grin was back when he headed back to the counter. By the time he reappeared, I had managed to subdue the goosebumps that had covered me at his touch.

"Why do you have two more cups?" I studied the tall man and how he filled out his white tee that more than hinted as solid muscle beneath.

His eyes were laughing at me again, and it hit me that he was several years older than me. "Because you're going to need more than that if you're hitting all the *one-o-one* exams."

I frowned, falling into step with him as he headed across the courtyard to the library. "You're not first-year?" I only took first-year courses, though admittedly, I took the maximum allowable for my semester, trying to get through them as fast as possible.

"Touching up previous experience." He slid a hand through his freshly shorn hair.

"What are you studying?" I sipped from the top cup, a balancing act I had perfected by the end of the first week of classes.

"Criminal Justice." He looked straight ahead, though a muscle ticked in his chiselled jaw.

Get a grip, Selena. He's only the hottest law student you've ever seen.

"Aiming for a police career? I would have picked you for Army, maybe."

"Been there, done that." He nodded, but the smile I'd already become accustomed to was absent, and I mourned it. Yet the serious young man made me more intrigued than ever. And a few months later, I experienced just what one of Liam's episodes looked like for the very first time.

But Liam's crash and burn was nothing like anything else I had ever seen. The man stood taller, became harder in his worst moments. And unless you were watching for it, or he let you in, the chances of anyone else knowing he was burning were easily less than zero.

I had seen Liam's crash-and-burn tactic too many times to count. He braved through it tougher than anyone, never ceasing to fight for what he knew he had to do — but he always came out the other side just a little more ragged.

Damaged.

Like part of his soul had died with the last flame of his fight.

His hand curled around me, tugging me into his chest. Liam's heart beat steady and strong against my cheek, his hand still at the back of my head where he threaded his fingers through my hair in a familiar comfort.

Ever the stoic, staid soldier, ready to sacrifice for the good fight.

But the fight that was coming wasn't good, and he wasn't a soldier. Not any more.

I squeezed his fingers where they tangled with mine and wondered how much this fight would take from him. What sacrifices he would make.

Liam released my hands, folding his arms around my back and let me cling to him.

The door to Cal's room opened. I heard it, more than saw it, with my head tucked into Liam's shoulder. I wondered if I had snored in the eternity that hadn't passed while we stood in a purgatory of our own making. I could hear the thoughts from every man standing around me: *if we had only*— but they were just regrets and rage that Liam reflected in his stance, in his stone-hard grip on my body. And the thought of my potential snoring became insignificant.

I lifted my head in time to see a woman in jeans and a sweater emerge from Cal's room, her hair pinned in a tight knot to the top of her head.

She motioned to us, but no one moved.

Liam shifted beside me. The woman caught the movement and motioned him over. He trailed his hands down my back to give a comforting squeeze — I wasn't sure if it was for him or for me — and stepped forward.

"Liam?" she checked a clipboard, not looking up to see his nod, "and Mila," she looked around.

Mila curled on Black's lap, her swollen belly taking up most of the space. Jenny held her legs across her own, and neither of them moved.

"Technically, you're not family, but you're listed with Mila on Callum' details. I'm going to take Callum into surgery soon. There's extensive damage to his lower torso and, of course, his leg. It will be a long procedure, possibly a few in stages, depending on how the first one goes."

"Again?" I whispered, forgetting I wasn't supposed to be listening, but every ear in the small group was trained on the doctor, and she had to know that. I swallowed the emotion and tried to focus. "I mean, haven't you already done that?"

The doctor shot me a quick look that reminded me of a certain judge. "Yes. We've done an initial round of surgery, but there is sufficient damage to warrant further work."

Liam rolled his shoulders, assessing her. "I'm not family."

"No."

"You shouldn't be telling me this."

"No," she agreed.

His lips pressed in a hard line, turning white on the outside. I watched the lines on his face smooth out. "How many hours?"

She lifted one shoulder. "Perhaps six. Give or take."

I blinked. A small hand slipped into mine. I jumped, expecting Mila's dark head of hair, but I came up to nose level with Jenny instead.

Cal had spent years visiting Jenny's foster daughter, Ashley. The daughter of the man who had hunted Cal and tortured Mila, but she was part of our rag-tag family now, not his. I knew Cal wasn't the only target, but I was also certain that he would be pleased with the outcome. Visiting Ashley had started as a need to fill the responsibility hole, but it had developed into a lasting friendship with both mother and daughter.

"I'll take Mila home," I said to no one.

Liam nodded.

It didn't get past me that he didn't ask the surgeon Cal's survival rate.

The doctor mimicked him, her gaze sliding over Mila's heavily pregnant form. "That would be best. Get her to rest, somewhere safe. We have phone numbers for you and for her. I'll call when he's in recovery, and you can come and see him."

Liam stared straight at her, unflinching when she held his hard gaze, but the lie in her face was obvious. He nodded again, his face set as he wrapped my hand in a death grip, the rest of us following him silently out of the hospital.

CHAPTER FOUR

LIAM

Selena dozed against my shoulder on the way back to Micah's. The convoy of Ubers trailed through Melbourne's industrial area where Micah had lived. Though the area was taped off, a badge flash gave us access to our vehicles — those that remained in any usable capacity — and trundled away to our respective places for the night.

To any prying eye, at least.

I left Danny on shift to watch Cal's door, not trusting anyone other than the immediate team. Too many years of betrayal had taught me that, and I refused to give Logan any more gimmes. Danny and Micah would work out a round-the-clock roster, and Ally and Brett could take their turns, too.

Each pair of drivers turned in a different direction after checking the vehicles for tracking devices. I refused to give Logan any further gimmes. He'd had his last, a costly one, and my brain had spent hours turning over every option as we waited by Cal's room for the unapologetic doctor to tell us to go home. That there was no hope.

I had held her lying eyes, gathered Mila alongside my incomplete team, and left the hospital, unsure if I'd see Cal alive ever again.

But my brain had churned during the trip back to Micah's place. I'd given Black one look, unsurprised when he handed me their phones.

"Take the girls. Go away. I don't care where, and I don't want to know where or hear from you again. There's only one time you bring them back." Another gaze held, just as hard, just as unflinching. And with just as little hope.

He nodded, an arm around Mila and Jenny. Mila's eyes turned from frantic to dozy when she was placed back in Black's care. She needed medical attention, but Black had already been through his own personal tragedies. There was no one I would trust her safety — and the baby's — with more than her handler.

Plus, Black had his own vendetta against Logan. The girls were safe with him.

"I'll collect Ashley," he said in a low voice, and I knew he was as conscious as I was of the risks of any plan made vocally. "You won't see us again."

I nodded, returning his clasped fist around mine, and the hint of a smile curled my lips. We had been blessed with an incredible team, and under the worst of urban battlefield duress, they stayed strong.

Black hadn't needed to give me platitudes that he would see me later. There was only one way this would all end.

Micah stood silent through it all, an arm around Jimmy and Laura, and I knew the boys would look after their girls — and vice versa.

I motioned the big cop over from where he picked at the remains of his home.

Completely covered in dust, Micah approached me, leaving Jimmy picking computer parts out of the rubble.

"You're on point. Take the investigation with Ally and Danny. Gather every single piece of evidence and get it to Selena. You don't stop until it's done, right?"

Micah cracked a rare smile. "We'll get everything to her. Will you come back?" his eyes turned sad, though the fixed smile remained.

Selena slipped against my side, her arms wrapped around herself as I drew her close. The combination of her strength and softness floored me, as always. I had never deserved her, but now I had a chance to earn something I had lost in the desert years ago.

I tucked her tight to my side, heading back to my silver sedan. A thick layer of debris-covered the roof. Scratches coated its once-sleek surface. Selena slipped silently into the passenger seat, trailing her fingertips over the cracks in the windscreen.

I put the car into gear, relieved when it started and took her home. The three phones crunched beneath my tyres as I headed away from the debris of more than one existence.

I undressed in a silent house. Neither of us spoke on the way home. Selena curled against the leather car door, turned away from me. Soft shivers wracked her small frame, and though I couldn't see her tears, I knew she suffered in her own small hell, the same as I did.

The gritty steering wheel dug into my palms as I consciously turned with care into the drive. My house stood dark, though it was only a few hours until the sun rose on a new day.

Mondays would be a constant reminder from now on.

A reminder that even when I thought we had won, when I thought we had all found *the end*, with our findings tidied neatly into an inescapable knot, that I had failed. And that the team I loved — my *family* — had paid for that lack of understanding.

I refrained from touching her. If Selena wanted to come to me, she would. And my own world of grief swirled from a grey haze in the shape of Micah's destroyed home and at least one destroyed life to an ever-deepening black of unfettered rage.

The door bumped beneath my hand, swinging open too gently for the fury simmering inside me. Inhaling her as she slipped past me, I let my hand linger lightly on her lower back. "Wait for me. I need to check the place first," I said in a low voice, trying not to close my hands around her in the event I hurt her in my cold rage." Then take a shower, and crawl into bed with me. Please," I added, waiting for her nod before I slipped inside the house, leaving her at the door.

My sweep didn't take long; it was my house, and I made a methodical check of the inside before looping around the perimeter to find her standing very still, more a statue of the woman I adored than the vibrant person I knew her to be.

We had never slept together — apart from a few evenings on the sofa in front of a movie that had ended hours beforehand — but I'd never invited her into my bed. Despite how close we were, she had never invited me into hers. I suspected it was bound by fear of rejection more than anything else on both sides.

I would never turn her down, but tonight, after everything that had happened, was different.

I was different.

She nodded, lifting a pale face to me that was tracked with tears. Even exhausted, the frayed edges of her so fragile, holding her together through the remnants of shock, she was still so beautiful.

Selena slipped into the house, her already bare feet padding softly up the stairs to the bedrooms. I let her go, heading into my own room, just across the hall from hers, and undressed in the dark.

By the time I sat on my bed, her door was closed. I took it as a sign that she wanted to deal with the night's events — the last eight years of events, the chaotic tragedy Logan spewed around us — alone.

Part of me ached, though another part of me knew it would make what I was about to do easier if she wasn't with me while I packed.

I threw out a few last messages to Danny, not having spoken to the young cop before we all parted ways. He would be a solid baseline for Micah to bounce his investigation off. Together, I had no doubt they would pull all the strings together I needed.

Flicking the screen to black, I slid it to the back of my bedside table and rose to sort out what I needed to hunt Wayde Logan. My hand was on the familiar, rough material of my empty rifle case. My fingers traced the familiar outline of my scope — cleaned regularly — when the slightest movement in my doorway caught my eye.

"You're going after him." There was no question in Selena's voice as she stepped into my bedroom. Her fingers trailed along the wall as she edged closer, her lithe body moving gently beneath her night shirt.

I blinked.

"Is that one of my old shirts?" The corner of my mouth curled as I dropped my hand.

Selena's head tilted to one side, deep chestnut curls tumbling over her shoulders. They retained their gloss, even in the darkness, and I itched to wind my fingers through them.

She nodded, stopping a hair's breadth from me. "I stole it out of your washing pile years ago. When this whole thing with Logan blew up, and he took the time that I wanted with you."

"*He* took the time?" I asked softly, trailing my hand down the side of the soft material, grazing her curves hidden beneath. That she chose her safety in wearing something at night that coated her in my scent brought on a possessive urge I'd all but hidden from myself about her — and a raging hard-on. "I've been here for any amount of time you needed."

"Which we both use working stupidly for jobs that don't leave anything for us," she huffed softly, her hips swaying beneath my touch to a tempo that was all her.

"That's a lot of time wasted." I dropped my hand and turned away from her, my heart burning from the inside out at her knowing gaze.

"Then don't waste the time we have left," she whispered.

"*Don't leave* is what I believe you mean," with my back to her, I pilfered through my things, but everything was where I remembered packing it away, only years ago.

My rifles were stored in a tall gun safe bolted to the cement floor in the basement where I had been building a boat that would never touch the water. I oiled and cleaned them every few months; the habit of a sniper's training drilled into me too many years ago. A short stint in the army that held the ramifications of a lifetime.

"Would you prefer me to tell you to go?" Selena's voice was light, though it trembled slightly at the end.

I gripped the open wall of the walk-in closet. "I don't want you to tell me to do anything."

The moment the words left my mouth, I regretted them. Not only were they hurtful, but they were also petty. I swung around to face her.

"Do you really want to do this alone, Liam? You don't even know about Cal—"

"I know that bastard will keep hurting us. I know that I can't ask anyone else to screw with their career, their *lives*, if I'm not prepared to do the same."

They would all do it if I asked. Getting them *not* to do anything was the hardest task. And so I gave them jobs and jumped in before they could screw their careers and their lives.

"There has to be another way to do this. The way we've always done things." There was a plea in her voice because of *him* that turned my blood to boiling.

"You mean the way that nearly got my brother killed." Or he could be dead. Cal was the closest thing to a brother I'd ever had, and a world without him in it wasn't my world. My chest squeezed painfully, and I refused to look at my phone on the bedside table.

Selena stood silent. It took every inch of frayed control to wait her out.

"He's not gone yet. You don't know what will happen, Liam—"

"If he's not, then it will be someone else. Do you want it to be one of the girls? You?" I raked my nails over my head, relishing the pain in my scalp. "I can't risk that. And I'm repeating myself."

"Yes, you're a broken fucking record on Wayde Logan. Please, Liam. Let someone else handle him."

"Are you going to walk away from this case? Drop it to Marcus? Leave the judge you've convinced to hear him, to convict him? That's a dangerous line on bribery all of its own, Selena."

Her palm cracked against my stomach. I tensed but managed not to flinch.

"You absolute bastard," she hissed through clenched teeth. "I do these things for you, to get you to come home. To give you what you needed!"

"You mean, to get what you needed," I leaned against the wall, letting my inner asshole show. If I didn't walk away from this thing with Selena not hating me, she'd end up trying to follow me, and I needed her as far from me as possible. "How's that working out for you?"

Because I fully intended to draw Logan to me, the biggest target on offer, now that Cal was down. Which meant I needed her as far away from me as possible.

Selena took a slow step forward, so I could see her coming. I pressed my hands to my thighs, knowing that if I touched her, I'd likely end up in my bed with her, and that was *not* how I wanted our first time to be. At this point, there couldn't *be* a first time.

Her hands smoothed over where she had slapped at me, working their way up my chest in an intimate gesture I had never allowed myself to indulge in with her. The press of her body against mine followed; every soft curve melded to the scarred facade of a hard man that only served to hide a mangled soul hidden deep within.

My breath gusted from my lips, the emotion flooding my system fully for the first time. I gripped her hard, my fingers sinking into her skin too tight, but she never complained; only curved closer to my body with her own and gave into the demands I placed on her.

When my arms relaxed a little, she tilted her head back. Dark eyes cast in shadow searched mine for an answer I couldn't give her.

Dark eyes that glistened with unshed tears.

Groaning, I dipped my head to kiss her, taking from her for the last time. Her tears brushed my cheeks, salt coating our lips as I pushed her back against the wall. My tongue danced with hers, and I withheld the edge of fury, of violence that filled me from her, savouring her taste.

Her skin was so soft beneath my hands as I bunched the material of my shirt she wore in my hand, grazing my knuckles over her stomach, to her hip.

She moaned softly into my mouth, her body undulating against mine. Our kisses softened, losing their desperation to be replaced with something deeper: all the words we had never said to each other. Selena's hands slid up my chest, wrapping tight around my shoulders as she clung to me, weathering my fear, the turmoil that roiled inside us both.

Slowly the tears stopped flowing, and the taste of our mingled terror and relief stung my lips. Selena rested her head against the hand that cushioned her head from the wall.

"You separated us. We're a team, Liam. We're stronger together."

The truth of her words hit me, twisting in my gut in a place already raw and flayed. If I'd thought the distraction would keep me from facing reality even for a moment, I was deluding only myself.

In an instant, the calm that flowed through me from the contact, the facade that I could protect her, was ripped away and replaced with the black ice that flowed swiftly through me. I pressed my palms against the wall on either side of her head, caging her in.

"We were stronger together until someone started picking us apart. Do you want me to leave Mila within that asshole's reach? Do you want to see her get taken, or the baby killed? Jenny, dead? Ashley gone? Because he will, Selena. That's what Logan does."

"I know, Liam," Selena traced the scar tissue that covered her from shoulder to wrist, her gaze flickering, "I have his signature carved into me."

I held her gaze in the dark light, wishing I could go back and take that shot for her a second time. "He's spent eight fucking long years playing with us, the mind fuck he's made himself famous for, laughing. Because he knew he had it all over us. For fuck's sake, he got to Mandy! That's who blew Micah's home apart, who ruined Cal. Mandy. Someone Cal met *before* any of us had heard of Logan."

Selena sucked in a breath. "Why didn't you say something? I could have—"

"Could what? She's dead. And if she isn't, then she will be soon. He'll see to that. The local cops have all the information I could give them, but whether they'll find her- well. It's Logan, isn't it?" I licked my lips, tasting her, fueling my rage with a need to protect them all when I clearly couldn't save fucking anybody. "He met her before Mila. Then Danny dated her after Cal. He's had her in our fucking back pocket for too long." My arms shook against the wall, and I held them still with effort.

"Then we do this together. We work it through together, Liam. We always have."

"And I've lost people, one by one, to him. Hell, he's been picking us apart from the inside all that time. And the number of times we should have lost someone? Black, Danny, Jimmy... you." I ran my fingers down her bare arm, where there was no shirt to hide the long scar. I knew she didn't try to hide it, but the questions from others had begun to bother her, and long-sleeved tops had become our new normal. The adjustments we all made.

"It's okay, Liam. I'm here," she whispered, cupping my face with warm palms, but everything inside me had hardened into the black ice that blocked her warmth from reaching me.

I laughed hollowly, the fear that twisted her beautiful features barely striking my numbed heart.

When I'd had to choose between her life and someone else's and the choice had been too easy. Using my weapon again, even after more than a decade away from the field, had been simple. It hadn't hurt me or bothered me. And that made me wonder if I had ever left the battlefield at all.

"I won't risk you or anyone else again," I snarled, digging my fingers into the plaster board behind her head.

Selena nodded, her dark eyes holding mine in the shadow, and I knew I was kidding myself if I thought I could hide anything from her.

"That's murder, Liam."

I snorted, not looking up. "That's not what they said when I got back from the desert. They gave me a medal for that. Remember?"

"I remember you refusing to go to the ceremony and throwing the box back at your superior officer."

"An officer who smiled because he'd never been deployed into the field and thought that being a survivor was a fucking *honour*."

"You survived." Her lips thinned, and I sensed a *chat* coming on.

"Not honourably."

Selena's fallback was always therapy.

What I had planned *was* therapy. It just wasn't what she had in mind.

CHAPTER FIVE

LIAM

Selena's arms slipped around my waist, pressing her soft body against my scarred and damaged one.

"You should go," I murmured, dropping my hand to the back of her head. "Get some sleep. It'll be dawn soon."

And there's so much to get through before that happens.

"You told me to come to you," she whispered into my chest, her plea edged with desperation.

I nodded, letting her believe what she wanted, tangling my fingers through hers, and led her to my bed.

Selena slipped between the covers, hesitating in the middle of the mattress. "Are– are you going to sleep?"

"Probably not." I tried to give her a crooked grin I knew would get a smile, but even that part of me was broken. I gave her a twisted grimace instead.

"Try?" she whispered, reaching out.

I hesitated for a long moment, wondering how long I would let the lie go on. Then I took her hand and slipped in beside her.

Selena's body curved around mine, her leg slipping over my hip as though she had always been there.

"Is this the first time you've been in this bed? My bed?" I frowned. The simple pleasure of having the woman I adored sharing my sheets, even fully clothed, was a joy I could take right now.

Cal was in the best hands possible, and Black would make sure the girls were safe. Danny would keep Micah and Ally focussed. Joey had been set his task. Everything was settled, but still, my mind refused to switch off. I set it on a different path.

"Nope." Selena snuggled into my side. "The last time I slept in a bed with you was when my roommate at uni brought home the entire band for a night's entertainment. I walked across campus in my pyjamas and crawled in with you."

"Hell, I'd forgotten that." My laugh surprised me.

Selena snorted, her lips brushing my chest. "I don't doubt it. You couldn't walk straight."

Selena's roommate had been a groupie to any band that played at the campus bars. "I remember you waking half of the college dorm because I was too drunk to open my door, and you nearly bashed it down. Good cuddles, though. And I'm glad you didn't stay with the rest of the band there."

Selena murmured something into my chest, wiggling a little.

I stroked down her back to find her shirt — my shirt — had ridden up. Rather than fight it, I slipped my hand beneath the material, stroking along her bare skin, memorising every inch of her curves with my hand. Hardening to the point of pain, I adjusted myself, shifting my leg against her to ease the craving, but it only made it worse when her knees parted, and she lounged over me, utterly relaxed and safe.

I swallowed every carnal thought I'd ever had about my best friend and tried to focus on what she was saying.

"To be fair, I think she meant to share them. Maybe," Selena said doubtfully.

"So generous of her."

"She was probably glad when I left so she could have them all to herself."

"Gods, girl. Stop." I pressed a hand over my eyes, but I was doubly glad Selena had ventured across campus to find my drunk ass. I didn't want to think about the alternative.

Selena giggled, shaking her head. Her curls draped across her back, trailing over my arm. I drew her in tighter, revelling in the soft sigh that brushed across my chest.

She traced unseen patterns on my stomach with her fingertips. "Where did you send Mila? She'll need to know about—"

"She'll know. And I asked him not to tell me. Or you," I shut the thought down before it could take root. "It's safest." I quelled the thought that Logan might be listening to my conversations. Hell, half the time, I felt like the man was inside my brain altogether.

Selena fell silent, still tracing over my abs with her fingertips. "You know, I have no idea if you're ticklish," she said softly.

"Now's not the time to find out," I warned her, catching her hand in mine. Her fingers wound between the roughened, calloused skin of my own, pressing our palms together.

Selena huffed a laugh, her breath gusting across my chest. After a time, her breaths evened, matching my heartbeat.

This is what I could have had, every night for fifteen years.

I knew without a doubt that she loved me and that I was safe with her. For a long moment, I closed my eyes and rested with a clear mind.

When Selena's breathing settled into a regular rhythm, I untangled my fingers from where I'd been massaging her scalp. Her body was soft and relaxed as she pooled into a pile of limbs and chestnut curls across my body.

Wishing I still had the tears to sting my eyes, I swept the hair back from her face, baring the long, gentle curve of her neck. My fingers lingered there until she shifted. Not wanting to disturb her further, I kissed her cheek and settled into packing the bare minimum of gear I'd need to hunt Wayde Logan.

Getting my rifles out of the safe in my basement wasn't an issue, but the heartstrings actually began to pull when I looked at the carcass of bones that was my ever-unfinished boat. Somehow, the exposed beams, partially planked that I'd redone a thousand times in ten years in an attempt at perfection, bowed me.

The police career had always been a bandaid fix. It was a temporary cover while I reclaimed some part of myself after the catastrophe in the desert. Then I'd met Selena, and suddenly I had a new mission to work towards — being worthy of the love and adoration she heaped on me daily. Love that was completely unearned.

And now, I was giving up everything I had worked for over the past fifteen years away. There was no coming back from what I planned. But Selena would be safe.

They all would be if I did things right.

Giving the boat in its unfinished condition a last, hard look, I snuffed out a dry laugh as I collected my things and flicked off the basement lights. I had never really left the battlefield.

I lay my weapons into their bags with care on my bedroom floor, extracting the bullets and magazines from a separate safe. Everything I did since I returned to the country had been above the law. I'd dipped a toe in the grey, but I had never actively crossed that unspoken, though clearly defined line.

A line I had taken to mean who I was.

I traced over the components of my dismantled rifle, over the padding that surrounded my scope. My fingers came away gritty. I rubbed them together. The fine grains that had travelled across oceans to come home with me fell back in their place in the darkness, unseen. I still heard the shouts of my men under fire, still clutched the too-heavy body of my spotter, limp in my arms.

The sand tearing at my skin in the wake of the gunfire that never touched me, but that downed everyone around me.

Sheets rustled behind me.

I closed my eyes briefly, pulling a thermal, black long-sleeved tee over my head. Another set of clean, black clothes and a day set for reconnaissance was already stashed in my larger rifle case. Wiping over my scope a final time, I shut the lid with a click, but it didn't matter; she already knew.

"You should be in bed," Selena whispered. The bed rustled more behind me before soft footsteps padded across the room to where I sat, my sniper paraphernalia scattered around me.

My phone vibrated on the side table.

I managed not to grab it. Just.

Selena had no such reservations, her movements too quick to grab my phone, to flick over the screen. Her silence ate at me, but I refused to look at her. Acknowledging her meant recognising the choice I battled against making, but my chance to slip away unseen, the coward's path that tempted me, flittered away.

I wouldn't have used it, anyway.

Cold palms slid around my waist, her body pressing to my back. Tremors shimmied their way along her limbs, her usual warmth a void that grew between us. I turned in her arms, cradling her face.

"Tell me."

"He's alive. He's in recovery."

"Thank God." I wrapped my arms around her, pulling her into my chest. She stared up at me, beseeching. I didn't look at her. "I'm not coming back to bed."

I'm not coming back at all.

The unspoken mantra hung between us, sowing its bitter seeds.

Selena stilled. "You're going to kill him."

It was a statement, and she didn't really need an answer.

"Yeah." I didn't pause in my preparations.

"Liam. I thought we were past this."

I barked a laugh. "Past what? The madman who has hounded every aspect of our lives for eight fucking years?" I raised my head, letting the deadness inside me bore into her.

She took a step back. "Liam—"

"Damn right, I'm going to kill him."

Feeling there was nothing more to say, I selected a pile of fresh Kevlar vests and tucked them into the top of the duffle bag. Straightening, I pulled my rifle kit from where I'd stowed it the night before.

Recognition flared in her eyes.

"You planned this. Last night."

"Yep." There was no point denying that, though a few moments of rest hardly qualified as *last night*. Still, it wasn't the right time to argue semantics. Or the right person to engage in it. I grinned, despite myself.

"This isn't how we do things. Liam, stop. You'll *become* him. Don't—" her hands dropped to my shoulders as her words died away.

"Don't what? Don't kill again?" I raked her with a hard stare she didn't back down from, though gooseflesh rose on her arms. "I've killed for you."

"That was in self-defence," she whispered.

Guilt sliced through me at the thought of making her feel blame for something that had never been her fault. I pushed it aside; at this point, if it achieved my ends, then I would use it, use anything to keep her safe.

"Then this is in defence of whatever will come next."

"It will be murder."

"No different from the desert."

"Stop." Her hands fell from my shoulders.

I straightened slowly, using my full height to tower over her. It wasn't something I used often, and I'd *never* done it to her.

"You want me to stop?" I watched the dark sparkle in her eyes melt away, replaced by something I hadn't seen in them before, and never wanted to see in them again. *Fear.*

Fear of me. I swallowed and ploughed on. "You want me to let it go? And wait for you, or Mila or the baby to be next? He will *never* let go. He will *never* stop. And I won't let him take any more from us."

My gaze burned into hers. My Selena. So beautiful. I reached out to touch her, to make sure she was real, but she batted my hand away. I let it fall to my side.

"This isn't what we DO, Liam!" she yelled. "We don't do what he does! This— it's not vengeance. It's revenge."

"Damned right, it's revenge."

"Then you do it without me."

"I wasn't expecting you to be part of it."

So you'll be safe because I pushed you away.

She took a hesitant step forward, then another.

She's afraid of me.

I took some perverse satisfaction in it, storing it in a dark place I knew I'd need to access later.

Her fingers brushed my cheek as she rose on her toes to kiss me.

Sweetly.

It was nothing that I needed.

I wound my fingers through her silky hair, crushing her mouth beneath mine in a brutal kiss, desire and violence igniting at the moment of contact.

She froze — an instant that lasted an eternity as I waited for her to push me away. A small mewl purred from her lips. I swallowed it as she melted beneath my touch. Letting my rage, my icy fury out in a slow release, I kissed her harder, finding a way to destroy what I'd treasured to push her farther away. Soft lips parted beneath mine as I swept my tongue into her mouth, devouring her, consuming her.

She needed to get away from me. To be safe.

Selena drew back with a cry, her lips dark in the pale shadows and swollen. My shirt fell over her hips where I'd yanked it up; the imprint of her curves seared into the palm of my hand. Her fingers brushed her lips as she stared at me in shock, her chest rising and falling too fast. Dark curls tumbled around her in a bedhead muss. Wide eyes stared at me, and I couldn't tell if she wanted to step into my arms and repeat that bruising kiss or run as far away from me as she could go.

I'd never wanted her more.

The desperate need to soothe her, to take her in my arms and love her like I should, ached through me.

But now, I couldn't.

"You– I—" tears welled in her eyes, tumbling unchecked over high cheekbones and swollen lips.

"Go, Selena," I gave her the final push, relentless. Ruthless. I had to be to get this job done. And it was my own damn fault I had spent too many years without her in my arms because I was afraid of ruining her, and now I was doing it anyway.

Shaking her head, soft curls trembling over her shoulders, Selena backed away until she hit the door. In a flash of salt and anguish, she was gone.

As her car squealed from the drive, I checked every component of my rifle, though I'd done it all in the hours before while she slept. Part of my mind roared at me, but it wasn't to chase her.

I love you.

Selena took my heart with her, but I couldn't afford to care about the consequences of my actions for myself. For her and the rest of the team, I wouldn't ask more than what I had offered any soldier.

When it was done, maybe. But I couldn't do this alone. There was one last person I needed to get me through this. To finish it.

I needed to find King.

CHAPTER SIX

SELENA

The road blurred beneath an unceasing rain of tears that coated my face as I drove away from Liam's house. My home. Even though I kept my townhouse after the message Logan sent that resulted in the long scar that striped my arm from wrist to shoulder, I had taken Liam's offer, given in his own, true style. A small key was in my handbag the day after I was released from the hospital, and I began to move my things into his house that day.

And nearly three years later, I barely thought of my townhouse, only returning on occasion for case files or older records.

I stood in the dark entrance foyer, gripping my phone. I had left Liam's house with only my phone and a fine tether on my sanity. The image of him stepping out of the shadows, scaring the life out of me to the point that I'd attempted to attack him with a move that he had given me. The memory brushed over me in the barest caress and was gone.

"Creeper," I could hear the echo of myself whisper, balancing my coffee stack while he grinned at me in a way

that made every inch of me dissolve on the spot. But that had been years ago, back when he had first invited me to live with him, after the last attack.

"Damnit, Liam," I whispered, rooted to the spot. I had no idea what to do next. All I could see through the sheen of salt was an empty existence without Liam by my side.

And a shadow approaching along my hallway.

A very solid, very real and hulking shadow of a man who most definitely was not Liam.

My feet were rooted to the floor in almost the exact spot that I had been in the last time Logan had sent his *message* to Liam. When Liam had broken my door down and shot my assailant.

I hadn't realised that he had killed anyone for a week before I'd read the police report and filed my own.

As my feet refused to work and my body froze somewhere between a fight and flight response to danger that Liam had spent years training me out of, I could think of only one thing.

Liam was right.

He had judged Logan and found all his flaws. For god's sake, he had found every one criminal's motivations, had flipped his own brother's loyalty. Now, he had taken Cal's obsession and transferred it to himself.

And I had doubted him.

The shadowy figure formed into a proper one, huge and hulking that filled my hallway. I slashed at the tears blurring my vision.

Hands caught my wrists, tugging.

I lurched, a scream dying a strangled death in my throat.

Another man, dark-haired, replaced the one in front of me. Darker, with closed features, sitting on my bed. The flash of a blade, cold slicing my arm open-

"Selena."

I blinked, and miraculously, the tears dried up. My jaw set, I forced my mind to focus through the frozen panic and lashed out with my fist in the general vicinity of the shadow's face.

He jolted, his head whipping to one side.

"Damn, you girls have got to stop maiming me." Warm, familiar tones robbed me of my fear, replacing it with an inconsolable need for security.

The voice might be familiar, but it wasn't who I needed right now. Warmth swamped me, flowing over me so fast my skin prickled, and the tears began again.

"Oh, god, Danny. I'm so sorry! I thought you were— were—" I choked again, and the words stopped while the tears flowed.

Broad arms engulfed me, platitudes murmured over my head, and for part of a second, I was safe.

"Liam sent me, babe. He wanted the house checked before you walked in." Wide, brown eyes that sat in an almost pretty face surveyed me, and I realised Danny knew I had left Liam in a mess.

"I— I—" The words stumped against my lips, unable to get out.

I left him in his house, alone.

I walked away when he needed me, even if he pushed me away.

I failed him.

Liam had always straddled a fine line between pushing the boundaries of law and making sure his boys followed it to the letter, never following him into the grey.

But this time, the murky mist of that line would engulf him, and I knew I wouldn't see him back on the right side of it again.

If he came back at all.

A new gush of tears rose, heat flushing my skin and prickling it beneath my clothes.

"You did what he intended you to do." Danny's voice was calculated, and I stared up at him.

"He's going to—" I coughed, choking on the admission, and started again. "This is going to end really fucking badly."

Danny's arms folded around me. "Amen to that, babe. I've checked the place. You're safe, and I'm here. Your shining knight for this evening. Let's get you to Marcus' house."

My world narrowed to a pinpoint with the man I adored at the centre. With a desperate rush, I wished I had pushed Liam harder, had spent the night wrapped in his arms, covered in his sweat.

The need to have something more of him to remember — more than the memories, but a deep, physical need to feel him embedded into my skin, something that time might not erase flooded me. Then, the guilt. If I had stayed for the night with him, would he stop? Could I have convinced him to stay, to stop, instead of running from him like a coward?

Doubt crashed over the guilt, wave after wave smashing me as I stood inactive, indecisive. I needed to be with Liam. We had always bounced ideas and cases off each other, had discussed fine points of cases from both his point of view and mine, and I knew he valued my opinion. But he had been set in his decision on this suicidal mission for vengeance, taking the brunt of everyone else's fallout. Like the sacrifice he never got to be as a soldier.

It should be his arms around me.

Instead, I was wrapped in the arms of a man who belonged to someone else, and even though he was my friend and I knew Liam trusted Danny implicitly, it felt wrong.

I pushed Danny away, noting that he let me go. The young cop was strong enough to lift at least a full-grown man. I was under no illusions that anything I did tonight was by his grace.

"You're not going to stop him." My words fell flat in my empty townhouse.

"What's to stop? That mad bastard might shoot me," Danny grinned, swapping the sting of his harsh words for humour — his usual MO.

But his words were true enough.

I nodded, collecting my things and let him lead me out to his car.

Mine was left parked outside my house, and I didn't know when I would return to collect it or live in my house again. If.

The engine of Danny's jeep purred beneath us through the inner-city streets of Melbourne, tracking to where my partner in our law firm lived. Danny pulled up at a red light.

I pressed my lips together, debating the words, but they tumbled out before I could stop them, raw and tangled.

"Can we go back ho– to Liam's, please? I've left a lot of things there. For work." It was a shitty lie, but I didn't care.

Danny half-grinned and flicked the indicator on. "Sure, babe."

His tone might as well have said, *it's your funeral.*

The house was dark though the sun had almost risen when we pulled up at Liam's house. The drive sat empty of cars, though his might still be in the garage. Maybe. Doubt bloomed in me with horrifying speed, threading through my chest, a corset of panic and terror. I clutched my house keys too tight in numb fingers.

Danny nodded in my peripheral vision. "Go on. I'll wait here."

"You don't want to check this house, too?" I asked in a light voice, proud that it was clear of tremors.

"Hell, no. I know what having my ass handed to me by that man would be like. He's all yours." Danny's arm slipped across the back of my seat, squeezing my shoulder in a gentle touch for such a big man.

I slipped down from his Jeep, padding barefoot across the road I had left less than an hour before. The edges of the keys bit into my palm as feeling returned. I pushed the door, and it swung open with zero resistance.

Tears burned the backs of my eyes, bile rising in my throat. I trotted into the hallway, noting the sheets on each of the mirrors in the hall that I had insisted he put in to give the place light, but he always covered up.

Maybe to hide the monster he believed himself to be. His self-fulfilling prophecy.

All they reflected was my panic as I tore through his house, screaming his name. My pace quickened, the trot becoming a run. Familiar rooms flashed by. I gripped the railing as I headed to his basement, flicking lights on as I went, but I already knew what I would find.

His half-finished boat was the sole occupant of a room too small for what he created there.

The tears welled and overflowed, blurring my path back up the stairs. I sat at the top, staring back through the hall to the open doorway. Danny's orange Jeep, still running, was visible through the long tunnel between me and my future. My brain tried to process the situation, but it got jammed on one brutal fact.

Liam's house was empty.

He was gone.

CHAPTER SEVEN

LIAM

Skyscrapers and suburban houses were traded for farmland and forest trails as I left everyone I loved behind. I hadn't stopped to say goodbye to Dad, though he would already be up, buying the morning's catch for the fish co-op from the local fishermen he had supported for the past forty years.

He wouldn't try to talk me out of my plan. He might even understand. But it was his disappointment I actively avoided, knowing I was giving into the primal, selfish urge for revenge rather than doing it the right way.

The way I had always done things, the way that had gotten a team of soldiers killed, leaving a sole survivor.

Well, two. But King had his own reasons for not being a part of that tour.

A pair of burner phones Danny had dropped at my doorstep sat in the centre console beside me. Just another reminder of how temporary any peace I garnered was likely to be.

I turned into Ben King's driveway, scattering chickens and loose gravel in my wake. The cottage was exactly as I remembered it. A shed off to one side, overfilled with bits of old cars tumbling from its permanently ajar doors. Random bumper bars and a miscellaneous car door collection sat rusting amongst long-term weeds that stretched tall seed heads to hip height.

The cottage looked just as it had when I was a green officer, coming for tea with King and his wife Mary, who insisted on hosting regardless of how awkward I felt. The walls were painted a fresh white, clean curtains hung in the windows.

But the rose garden out the front was bereft of colour, rosehips poking past blackened leaves their only decoration.

I parked to one side of the circular area at the front of the house, leaping up the short flight of stairs to the verandah in a bound. The screen door rattled beneath my fist. I pulled it open, knowing King had been formidable for never locking anything, and rapped on the heavy wooden door instead.

"Ben!" I yelled, scattering the chickens again. They landed behind me, filling the air with a gentle mumbling of clucks. "Oi!" I tugged on the door handle, surprised to find this one stiff, and locked from the inside.

"Yeah, yeah, yeah." His mutters reached me faintly. "I don't take callers, I hate the internet, and if you're selling solar panels, you can fuck right off."

The door opened. I squinted into the dim light beyond. "Ben?"

"You." The door thumped against the wall as it opened fully, and my gaze dropped to waist height as Ben wheeled himself out into the sunlight.

"That's new," I stared at my first spotter, the consummate survivor missing one leg in a wheelchair I didn't remember him being in. "What happened, old man? Another tour?" I reached down to hug him.

Ben slapped my back too hard. "Tour of the city hospital. Cancer's eating this bastard alive," he grinned, a slightly mad glint in his eye that told me he battled on as he always had.

"Nothing's changed about you, then." I turned in the direction Ben indicated, walking down a short ramp that led off the edge of the verandah. New planks clashed with old in a battle of peeling paint and fresh lacquer.

"Same old," Ben snorted, following me to the yard. Chickens clucked around him, pecking at his carpet slipper. He slipped a hand into his pocket, withdrawing a handful of seed and scattered it around the chair, making sure there was enough for each chicken. "And that's all, ye greedy buggers." The faint trace of his accent took me back to days roasting in the desert beneath a blanket custom covered with sand and scrub, waiting for my mark.

"You're still the best I had ever worked with, you know," I remarked.

A chicken dashed at Ben, flapping madly. He caught it in mid-flight and settled it on his lap.

"You need someone again? I thought you left all that behind." He squinted up at me.

I leaned against the hood of my car, sliding my legs down a little. "Shit's hit the fan. I need a spotter." I shrugged. "I was hoping for you, but—"

"Not mobile, but still got a good eye."

"Recommendations?"

"Fuck, boy. How deep have you buried yourself?" Ben grumbled, patting his chicken.

"Deep enough I won't see daylight from it at the other end. But it needs to be done. Got anyone you want to throw under the proverbial bus?"

Ben tilted his head down and studied his chicken.

I've come to the wrong place. There are ghosts here.

The thoughts sprang across my mind, unbidden. Ben had been a soldier, spotting me on over twenty missions before he got the call that he had lost Mary in a car accident while he was across oceans, leaving a small child behind. It was the last mission Ben had done with me.

My breath hitched, and I swore at myself in my head. "I'll check in with a few other ex-grunts, Ben. You've got peace here."

I was halfway around my car when he broke his silence.

"I've got someone who's bored and will do the job for you. Probably save your high-class ass at the end of the fight, too."

I snorted. "Since when have you been the fairy fucking godmother?"

"Since I'm sending you to my son."

Gunshots ricocheted back at me across the open-air rifle range. The Combined Arms Training Centre — CATC — sat ninety minutes north of Melbourne. I leaned back against the office wall, the only shaded spot. An old trainer had signed me in at the gate with a promise for a beer at the Officer's Mess later on.

A lone soldier lay on his stomach on a tarp, firing from a tripod. His targets stood out in the distance across the bare paddock that bore evidence of ordnance practice. I squinted at the far one, a wavering speck in the distance, maybe a kilometre out.

It was a stretch, even for a sniper, and from the little research I had managed to compile on Ben's son, King Jr had a decent track record in his short career. His movements were fluid as he made his shot, noting his adjustments as he manually calculated elevation and windage.

The time he took, his relaxed posture, told me he had done this a thousand times or more. Finally, he packed up his kit, dismantling his rifle with care but also with an efficiency I admired, and slung the case across his back.

He walked past the admin building without a glance. I let him get a few paces in front of me.

"Noah."

He turned on his heel, the shaven blonde head so reminiscent of Cal that it rocked me for a moment. A wary look crossed his tanned skin.

"Who are you after?" he asked, his stance still casual, though his grip on his rifle case strap tightened.

"You're Ben King's son?" I asked, pushing away from the wall. The young man stood a good foot taller than his father, but he had the hint of laughtrer in his gaze I knew could turn hard just as fast.

The kid had to be twenty, maybe twenty-two. Which meant he had been around five when his mother was killed, and his father resigned from active service to look after him. He should have been an Army brat with a chip on his shoulder, but instead, he wore his uniform well. Comfortably. Far more so than I had at his age.

Before I was sent on a desert tour and came home with a false pride in the uniform as my memoir.

A badge stitched to the sleeve of his shirt showed a pair of rifles overlaid at the barrels, with an *S* sewn through it. I stared at the familiar stitching, knowing how it felt between my fingers. A Crossed Rifles Sniper badge was worn with honour — the highest accomplishment awarded for his specialization — and completed my assessment of the kid.

"Is Dad okay?" he asked, a furrow in his brow and took a step back toward me.

"Ben's fine," I raised my hands, "didn't mean to panic you. He sent me your way."

"Yeah? What's the old man want?" Noah King's lips thinned into a straight line.

I raised an eyebrow. "You don't get on?"

"Who are you again?"

"I've got a job. Are you bored here?"

I had the room set up by the time Noah King knocked on the rental unit door I had secured for the time being. Temporary enough to move on a day's notice, but it gave me a place to leave my kit while we were on reconnaissance duty.

Everything I needed was laid out on the floor in order. My surveillance equipment was set up on the small coffee table in a similar fashion. Giving it all a last glance, I crossed the small room and opened the door.

Noah King stood in the doorway, bronze-skinned and blond, shaved head rocking the twin image of Cal. I gripped the door frame tight and tried to smile.

"Brought you a present." He hefted a rifle case from his shoulder and pushed past me, surveying the small room. "Hell, man. I don't share beds."

"I usually ask my presents to wear less," I shot back.

"What can I say? I look good in hot pants." His back to me, he flicked me the bird over his shoulder.

I snorted. As an army brat turned soldier, he would have been around the type of banter his father and I breathed.

"Thanks for coming, Noah. I know you came because your Dad asked you to—"

"Piss off with the speech." He sat on my bed, throwing my paperwork into disarray. "Let's get a few things straight. My name's King. Nothing else. I'm here because I don't have a mission, and I thought it would be fun. And that's the first time I've spoken to Dad in a year."

I raised both eyebrows as he kicked off his boots. "You prefer your father's callsign when you don't get on with him?"

"It's my damn callsign. You'll want to look at those." He nodded to the rifle bag in my hand.

Not taking my eyes off the unruly kid on my bed, I unzipped the case, extracting two spanking brand new, high-powered rifles.

"Did you sign these out on your own? They look like they've hardly been fired." I sniffed the barrel. Maybe a few times. But they still smelled like the firearms equivalent of a new car.

"I know the girl at the store. She did me a favour."

"Favours lead to more favours and favours owed. You want to be careful with those."

King was silent for a long moment. "I got her brother out of juvie last year. Cleaned him up. She owed me."

"Fair enough." Juvenile prison usually led to repeat offenders. If King had invested time with the kid, it meant he saw projects through, despite his shit-talking.

"These are perfect." I studied the pair of high-powered sniper rifles, pristine scopes to match, and an assortment of tech, which included a spanking new Black Hornet Nano UAV — a miniature drone Danny had mentioned to me a week ago in the hopes of getting one for the unit. I ran my fingers across it, swallowing bitter seeds at the reminder. "Thanks for the care package."

"Not a problem. I picked them out from what Dad said you'd need."

"He'd know," I put the rifles carefully back in their place and checked the ammo pouch. "I remember you, running about in a nappy behind the shed. Always getting into some sort of trouble."

King groaned and flopped backward on my bed.

That one's yours now.

"You know how fucking old you sound, man? Like every fucking solder through eight bases around the country hasn't said that to me."

I huffed a laugh before I could stop myself. "Fair enough. This is what I have planned."

Half an hour later, King was neck-deep in files, picking out fine points and holes in my plans as he went. The deja vu sense of Cal mixed with Danny rocked me more than once, and I was glad Ben had sent me in the direction of his son.

If Noah King was anything like his father, then he would be an enormous asset.

"Alright. We try this your way, and if it fucks up on you, we can reverse it, and I'll take point, be your sacrifice. You take back up. You're already too invested in this to do it right." He leaned back, his arms behind his head as he stretched and caught my eye.

I managed to bring my jaw back to its usual position. "Uh, sure," I said, caught off guard. It had only happened a handful of times, and I didn't like it any better than the last one.

King grinned. "Not what you were expecting?"

I resisted the urge to roll my eyes at the younger man, but the freshly-shaved blond head, the swagger, and the mischievous glint reminded me all too well of another man.

"You– remind me of someone," I hedged. "I'm sure you'll fit in just fine." Sarcasm edged into my words.

King grinned. "Sorry, dude. I don't do older men."

I snorted, looking away. King would fit in just fine.

CHAPTER EIGHT

SELENA

Marcus demolished his plate of sauteed mussels on toast while I pretended to pick at my own food. Liam had been gone for two days. I had no idea where he was, though I had a damn good idea what he was doing.

Sunlight streamed through enormous, arched windows that lined the street front of a restaurant I had never been in, its filtered rays too weak to warm my back. I sat in a fancy, overpriced restaurant in a tailored suit as white-gloved waiters moved around the few patrons filling the large space. I dressed as n automaton every morning, brushed my hair and put on makeup, all the while feeling the fraud growing inside me at the act.

We hadn't caught Logan, he wasn't in jail any longer, and I'd lost Liam. That I might have been able to take the case to trial earlier ate at me. I added my own failure to Liam's perceived ones in a nightly pity party kept at bay during daylight hours only by the constant activity around me. If I stopped, the facade would crack, and then I would be useless to anyone at all.

Logan's case was passed over from Micah and Danny to a team who knew nothing about the madman in a blindsided sweep of bureaucracy that wasn't entirely unexpected. *Failure* and *overdue* were terms that were thrown around a lot. I praised every law book that the boys kept me in their loop — and their ongoing investigation, despite orders to the contrary in Liam's absence.

The bureaucracy of the place would have filled Liam with a fire to incinerate the bullshit talk the moment walked back in. I swallowed too-hot coffee, ignoring the streak of pain.

But he's not coming back.

Joey had disappeared off the edge of the map, which more than concerned me. What if Liam had been right about him the entire time? But Micah, who was supposed to be babysitting him, just shrugged the questions off when I asked about the whereabouts of Logan's baby brother.

"Eat, Selena," Marcus prodded me, inhaling the last of his brunch.

It was a habit we had made years ago when we had first partnered up to create our law firm. An eleven o'clock late breakfast/early lunch was scheduled, depending on who you talked to. Marcus knew I would exist entirely on a diet of black coffee if given a choice, so five days a week, he stuffed food into me.

But with the mess of our lives, the case we spent years putting together damaged beyond any form of repair, and Liam deserting us all, I had less appetite than usual.

A waiter passed, and I tapped my mug, silently asking for a refill.

He took one look at me and was back in an instant, leaving the coffee jug on the table.

Marcus thanked him for me as the neverending stream of tears threatened. Again.

"You don't need to be with me every moment, Marcus. Though I'm glad of your hospitality," I added hastily, in the event I sounded ungrateful when the eternal bachelor had opened his home to me.

"I know you don't want a babysitter, but I've seen that man of yours. I wouldn't want him coming after me," Marcus laughed too loudly.

I winced, gripping my mug with whitened knuckles. Hot liquid slopped over the side, dripping down the back of my hand. I tried to feel the burn, but nothing seemed to happen.

"That's not– he's not—" I swallowed past the lump blocking my airway. "You can't say—" Everything burned, except for my hand. I let the words hang over the table, a mist of desperation amongst a cloud of chatter and heady scents that filled my head with nonsense.

A smooth hand covered mine. I looked up in surprise as Marcus shifted his chair around the table to sit beside me, still holding one hand as he pried my mug from the other.

I relaxed stiff fingers, flexing them. With renewed circulation came the burning pain.

Finally.

Marcus pressed an ice-water glass to the back of my hand. "Hold it there for a bit," he said kindly, patting me.

Biting back a totally inappropriate laugh that may or may not have bordered on hysterics, I nodded, retaining some minute degree of decorum in a public space.

The nights had passed tear-stained and sleepless in Marcus' spare room. The walls were thin in his apartment, and I was under no illusions that Marcus hadn't been an incidental third party to my grief for a still-living man. I just hoped I hadn't kept my business partner awake for too many hours during the quiet of the night when sleep eluded me. Besides, I needed him.

As impractical as it sounded, someone had to keep the firm running.

The waiter cleaned our plates away. I blinked as a takeaway cup was pressed into my hands, filled with the remnants of my liquid breakfast.

"Thank you," I whispered, horrified at the thought of breaking down in such a public space. "For everything. You've opened your home to me, let me stay while I'm an utter mess, screwed with our casework—"

Marcus' arm wrapped around my shoulders. "Shh. It's fine. Stay as long as you like. I actually like having a woman in the house."

I jerked a little at the contact, looking up. His dark head was too close, pale blue eyes startling in a darker face.

His gaze dropped from my eyes for a moment, and he leaned in. When I thought he might kiss me, he deviated to pressing his lips to the top of my head instead.

He paused above me, and the line of my shoulder went taut, that instinct that told me I was in trouble kicking in.

"Why don't you take a different sort of case? I've laid some out for you for when we get back," Marcus said softly, and I could hear the smile in his voice.

"I get the toddler distraction option?" I tilted my head back and grinned at his technique, but the comment was lost on the perpetual bachelor. It wasn't a bad option; without the Logan case to focus on, I was a little at loose ends, and I appreciated the gesture.

With a slightly perturbed expression, Marcus squeezed my shoulders again then released me, striding across the room to settle the tab.

My skin prickled again as I rose, brushing non-existent crumbs from my black suit pants, but it wasn't from Marcus, this time.

More the feeling of eyes on *me*.

I slowly revolved on my heel, my gaze sweeping the streetscape, then the building opposite. A shadow that might have been a figure in one of the windows shifted in its depths. A passing truck marred my vision, startling a flock of pigeons into the air, and by the time it had passed, the window was empty.

CHAPTER NINE

LIAM

I swore, shifting to duck away from the window. Even though she had turned on some instinct, looking for me, I didn't think Selena had seen me. Yet something had attracted her attention to the office building opposite where she and Marcus had breakfast.

The empty conference room had been easy enough to slip into. Not having anything on Logan's immediate location, I had taken the opportunity to check on Selena. After two days apart, I realised how much physical contact I had with her. How much I missed it.

Grazing her hip when I made her coffee, tugging on her curls when she berated me for not getting any sleep, though she had less, waiting for me. Kissing her, when it got too much, and I couldn't hold it back anymore and had to taste her, feel the warmth of her in my arms.

When Marcus had laid his hands on her, it had taken every restraint not to hit the street level and confront the bastard. I craved her touch, the corve of her beneath my palm. The rifle in my hands felt too hot, and for a single instant, I'd drawn a bead on his back, my finger brushing the trigger before I'd dropped the weapon, disgusted with myself. The same instant Selena had searched the window like she'd sensed me, or maybe just danger. I'd become the threat she feared.

I should have sent her off with Black.

But he already had Jenny, Ashley, and a pregnant Mila to deal with. Which was enough for any man.

I grinned and hoped he had enough room for the coral of ponies Ashley towed around in a puff of unicorn glitter.

I watched Selena join Marcus at the till, where he paid for their lunches. A moment prior, he had leaned in to kiss her head in a gesture that screamed intimacy. His hand brushed over her back, guiding her out the ground floor of the hotel where they had eaten. My nails bit into my palms as I clenched my fists, wishing Marcus' throat was between my fingers.

Forcing a long sigh, I relaxed my hands with effort. I had put her in with him and walked away. If she allowed someone else to touch her, then it wasn't her fault; that lay strictly with me.

My burner phone buzzed on the small table next to me.

I frowned. Only two people had that number.

King: Stop perving on your girl.

...

...

I waited for the three little dots to stop wiggling, not bothering to reply as I kept my gaze fixed on Selena.

King: Want me to shoot him?

I'm good at close range.

The laugh that burst from between my tight lips surprised the hell out of me. Grinning, I watched from the window as he walked a few paces behind Marcus and Selena, making a not-so-subtle gun with his pointer finger and his thumb aimed at Marcus' back.

The kid was rubbing off on me.

"You could bring her with us. Though I might get jealous if you look at her more than me." King tossed imaginary hair over his shoulder, preening.

"Fuck off," I muttered, changing lanes through city traffic as we headed into a commercial area.

Brantley Gilbert's *You Don't Know Her Like I Do* tore holes in my heart at the thought of leaving Selena with Marcus. He had been the logical choice, but his total lack of ability to protect her bothered me more than anything. I needed to split King in two to put a detail on her, as my boys were already working around the clock to cover Cal at the hospital and their own duties.

Danny had messaged me through the location of a partial hit from CCTV, a location which I had confirmed with Joey. A warehouse behind a vet's surgery on the edge of the city. It reminded me forcibly of where Cal had met Mandy, where I could now look back and see the beginning of the trail with Logan.

As uncomfortable as the thought made me that we were walking into another Logan-themed set-up, at least we had a starting point.

All I had to do was find Logan, set up the shot, and take it.

What sounded simple was likely to be several days of reconnaissance without showing any sign of our presence. In an industrial area, with fewer people around and lower buildings, that was harder than it seemed.

If Logan was there at all.

Doubt rose in me; what if it was Joey that the partial image had picked up? He had a similar facial structure to his brother. And I wouldn't put it past Logan to have someone physically alter something in his brother's face to make him fit the profile needed.

A car crossed lanes in front of me. I slammed on the breaks, cursing myself for not paying more attention. The twin distraction of Joey and Selena could cost us everything. If I lost my shot at Logan now, the thought of him roaming free to distribute his personal brand of terror over the lives of the people I loved most sickened me.

Which meant I had to let one distraction go, and it couldn't be Joey.

I swore again, weaving through traffic.

"You know, you've missed your calling as a speed demon. Yeah, I know, fuck off," King waved me down before I could cuss at him, too. He looked at me sideways, a grin tugging at the corner of his mouth. "Got a limited vocabulary, don't ya?"

It came out in a long drawl, custom-designed to irritate. I resisted punching him, only so I didn't crash the damn car. And after the two hours I spent going over it top to tail to ensure there were no devices planted in it for any purpose, I was loath to give the thing up.

"Get out," I pulled over, the coupe tilting a little as I drove up the gutter and braked with a jolt.

King turned to me with wide eyes and both hands up. "Wait, man. I was joking."

"We're walking from here." I stared at him for a long second, then grinned. King's startled expression was gold. "Fuck, you made that too easy. Green prick," I added for good measure, knowing the jibe would rile him.

King glared at me, grumbling in a dark tone as he climbed out of the car. He joined me at the back of a warehouse that had seen better days several decades ago.

"Fine. What are we doing all the way back here?" King folded his arms, squinting into a shadowed interior reeked of stale piss.

"I need a place to hide the car, and we need a reason to be here. A reason that lets us be present and remain unseen. *If* he's here."

"What, as fucking drug dealers?" King nodded to a pile of rubbish clustered around one corner of the dilapidated building. A used syringe sat on top. He edged away from it.

A grin split my face. "That'll do just fine."

I peered through the rifle scope King had provided in his care package, watching the target address from the top window of the warehouse. The place was filthy and had recently been home to at least one occupant with questionable hygiene, from the not-too stale scent of urine that pervaded the place.

"Got anything?" King's voice asked softly in my ear.

I leaned away from the window, making sure to stay in the shadows this time. "Not yet. You?"

"Car just pulled up. Can't see anyone– and another. He got a brother that looks like that photo?" King asked from his place on the other side of the block Joey had given us.

He got ground duty because the chance of Logan recognising him as working with me ranged from unlikely to non-existent.

"Yeah. Anyone with him?" I couldn't see any movement from my angle.

Damnit. I need to be in a different bloody building.

I sat back, stretching stiff knees and wiggled my toes. Circulation increased until my feet were sweaty, pouting me back into the soldier adage that if there wasn't anyone pretty enough to care around, then I didn't either.

"Yeah. Couple of thugs... chick with a shitty red dye job."

Mandy.

"Yeah, that sounds right," I said, my throat tight. I flicked off a text to Danny without looking at my phone and tossed it to the floor.

My earbud filled with the slightest amount of static.

"You want to add her to your list?" King asked lightly, "between her and Marcus, it's getting long."

I huffed a laugh. "Yeah, in my spare time."

"Okay, got your target. Blue suit, stupid out of place. More like a real estate agent than a bank robber turned murderer."

"Yeah, that's him." Energy filled me to overflowing and sank just as fast. I squeezed my fists together, imagining Marcus' face when I punched him. If I was going to spend life in jail after this, then I would make sure I'd get my fist in his face first.

A wave of sickness swarmed over me, eating at the edges of my remaining conscience.

What the fuck is wrong with me?

I'd do what I had to do, and that was all. Walk into the local police station, hand them my rifle and my badge. Anything to keep them all safe.

To keep Selena safe.

The thought of her burned the back of my throat. I wished I had kissed her softly the final time I had seen her, had loved her the way I'd always wanted to. Maybe it was a good thing that I hadn't; she wouldn't be stained by me. Maybe Marcus was a better choice, after all. Someone who could provide the comfort she needed, someone she could trust.

"You alright in there?" King asked, puffing slightly.

"The fuck are you doing, getting laid?" I threw the vulgar comment in more as a distraction for myself than to get a bite from King.

"They got too close. The brother eyed me. Talked loud on my phone, swore a bit about bitchy exes and kids and jogged away. He yours?" King switched topics faster than I usually did.

I grinned. The kid had more smarts than Ben ever had. But his father's strength had been loyalty and a cool head under direct fire. I wondered if his qualities had been passed on to the next generation.

"Why do you ask?" I forced myself back into the present.

"Dunno," King's breathing slowed. "Something about the way he hovered when he saw me."

Shit.

"Did Logan see it? The brother's reaction?" I snapped. Damnit. I should never have sent Joey back in.

Joey was worse than borderline scum, but he had actually tried to come back from it, from what I could see. He had even started at a real job if I was able to believe in his actions. But that might have been his fear of me, overriding his fear of his brother.

He'd always said Logan would kill him unless he could convince the psychopath that he was a turncoat twice over.

I cursed again.

"What?" King's voice was slightly louder, the rear door to the warehouse opening. I tensed until I recognised his figure halted in the centre of the open space.

I took the stairs one at a time, letting the thought turn over in my mind, furious with myself that I hadn't considered it before.

"What?" King watched me take the bottom stairs two at a time with a wary look in his blue eyes that reminded me far too much of Cal.

"I sent Joey back in with his brother. He flipped for me, and his job was to convince Logan he never had. Played the role and tested the waters. But he was fucking terrified of it, terrified Logan would kill him." I paused for breath.

"And there he is, without a mark on him," King finished the thought for me.

I nodded, sliding my hands into my jean pockets. "Without a mark on him."

I stared past King's shoulder, wondering how else I could possibly fuck up this operation before it even got started.

CHAPTER TEN

LIAM

Cole Swindell's *You should be here* played softly through the car's speakers. I sang a few disjointed bars, thinking of Cal as I drove to the top of a hill that overlooked the warehouse Logan appeared to frequent. King rode shotgun in a seat that should have been occupied by a body that looked far too much like the brother I missed almost as badly as I missed Selena.

A meeting place, a drop, a planning room. Whatever the hell Logan was doing there didn't bother me. As long as he *was* there, could be located there when I needed to find him was all that mattered.

Next to me, King leaned back in his seat, his eyes closed. Cal had always been up for shenanigans ever since our uni days, but this might be too much, even for him. With a baby on the way, he might have been less cautious than I suspected, considering the perpetual obsession he and Logan had with each other. Would I risk him with Mila waiting for him at home? That was the appeal of King.

We were all too invested in the hunt for Wayde Logan, the ongoing case that never seemed to quit.

King had no such issues with it.

As if I'd summoned him, the doppelgänger of his father twenty years ago leaned forward, switching the song to something with a rapid beat that rapped an incessant tattoo inside the front of my skull.

I glared at him.

"What?" King shrugged. "He's not dead yet."

I didn't bother to answer him, my eyes returning to the road.

It irked me that mini-Cal was right.

"Fine." I pushed the word out through gritted teeth, pulling into a parking area at the top of the hill. But unlike every day this week, it wasn't deserted.

Balloons and a bouncing castle occupied the space we had skirted out as a potential platform with prime real estate position for the shot.

"The problem with public spaces," King leaned out the window, peering about. "That one." He pointed to a building with a clear line of sight to Logan's local haunt as a secondary option, seeing as the hilltop was out.

"Top of that one, you think? Or the window inside?" I craned over his head. Hell, the kid was almost the same height as Cal.

"Rooftop. Gotta be. Next floor down impinges on your view. You're good to shoot at what, a hundred metres dead on?" King raised an eyebrow that made him worthy of his callsign at that moment.

"Arrogant little fuck, aren't you?" I eyed him, but to my surprise, it didn't come paired with the surge of dislike I expected.

"Take after the best," he grinned.

"Alright. Let's get this done so you can go home."

Thankfully, King said nothing as I pulled away from the hilltop, though my car was covered by bubbles and party glitter by the time we made it to the bottom of the hill.

The top of the building was frigid.

"You need to take your shot from inside, old man?" King asked, working through calculations, though the rifle he had provided did the job for him. I appreciated that he didn't rely on the tech to get him through. And we had time — plenty of it — before Logan arrived.

"If my edge is dulled, it's from working with braindead politicians and driving a desk for too many years." My lip curled. That position had been a thinly-veiled push from the military to move out before they discharged me as a broken weapon.

I had always hated working upstairs from Cal's team. Selena had suggested it — with *suggested* used in the most forceful and brutal way a woman could use to get what she wanted. Which apparently, was me joining the braindead brigade at a conference table for more hours than I would ever care to add up.

The thought of her panged in my chest. I pushed the emotion aside before I could study it properly. It had no place here, not until it was done.

"Your moral compass is all kinds of sideways, Liam." King shook his head, adjusting his calculations to include the short drop.

I hadn't realised I had spoken aloud. Pressing my lips together, I looked over at the young soldier, and this time, it wasn't Cal he reminded me of.

I look at you, and I see who I was. Who you might become.

And I hoped to any god that's listening that he would make better choices than I had.

Swallowing back the memory of what it was like to spin shit without the memories jam-packed behind a thin veil of bitterness, I lowered my eye to the scope.

"You can stop fussing, junior. I've got this."

The funny thing about words like that; they often ended up being a self-fulfilling prophecy.

Sniper work rarely looked anything like how Hollywood projected it. The hours waiting, barely pissing or using a plastic bottle in case you miss your mark while you're off twiddling your thumbs were never incorporated. The boring hours of waiting, lost in your own head of exit strategies, and consequences and talking yourself into and out of the shot two dozen times.

I'd given up counting the pebbles that bit into my stomach when I couldn't remember which ones I'd already noted anymore. And at the end of the day, it came down to what little circulation remains, a focussed mind, and a window of fewer than ten seconds.

The car pulled up as I was wiggling my toes for the umpteenth time. I stared through the scope at Joey as he exited the vehicle wearing a pale grey suit that made him look weedier than the gangly, underfed man already was.

The change in clothes took me aback; was Logan setting his brother up as an easy target? Maybe there was a reason the skinny man wasn't damaged — not visibly, at least. I hadn't shared our plan with anyone, and King had left his phone back at the training compound at Puckapunyal.

Joey slipped his hands into his pockets, and a moment later, another car pulled up behind his. A group of men clambered from both cars, a tactic I had seen before; security huddling around their prize, escorting it into a building. Extra targets and distractions to remove focus from the real mark.

Blue suit or black suit? I scoured the small crowd, but I couldn't identify Logan in it.

What are you wearing to your own funeral, motherfucker?

Sweeping the area with the scope, I panned back just in time to see him emerge from the back of the first car. I frowned; two things stood out of sequence, and that really bothered me.

Logan stood, his hands outstretched when the crowd descended on him. He shook his head, his back to me.

A clear shot, perfectly in the open, as though it had been planned.

I hesitated.

My ten seconds wound down and passed. I held my breath, something I had never done before taking a shot.

King shifted next to me but said nothing.

As we passed that ten-second mark that I set for myself, Logan swivelled on his heel, resting his forearm on the roof of the car he had gotten out of a few moments earlier, which could have been hours.

He looked straight at me, and I still didn't take the shot, my finger hovering just over the trigger.

A faint smile played across the asshole's lips, and he raised one hand in a wave.

Then very deliberately, he turned his back to me and walked away.

I watched him enter the shadow of the building, walking down the row of thugs who gave him a wide berth and step inside the safety of the building.

My breath whooshed out in a long breath, and I sat back, methodically dismantling the weapon.

King looked at me, a faint frown across his brow.

"Pack it up. We're out." I placed the last pieces inside the case and secured it, slinging the case over my shoulder. "He knew we were coming."

King gave a sharp nod, collecting everything with brutal efficiency, removing our presence, and walked across the rooftop without another word.

I watched him retreat, wondering if I had recruited a traitor instead of a soldier.

Methodical was the theme of the day. I cleaned every surface, wiped down walls, cleaned the guns and wiped those down, too. Everything unfired.

"Take them back with you." I passed everything to King, who watched me through clear eyes. He made no move to take the case from me. "Take the damn thing before I throw it," I growled.

"You've given up? I mean, good for you, but that was a clean shot. I know what your path was for yourself, so regardless of what he knew, you've changed plans. Might not be your best course of action." He slipped the strap from my hand and looped it casually across his chest.

I stared. "What the fuck is wrong with you? That was a set-up. And the only person who picked the building was you."

"Fuck, man, don't waste your breath blaming me for your midlife incontinence. I mean, it's a regular problem, but I figured you'd be past that." He knelt and began to unpack everything I had already organised.

"Put it away and get out. If I see you again, I'll shoot you," I snapped the words off at the end between my teeth.

King ignored me. "You know what? I reckon it is that lot you mentioned. The braindead politicians. Too much time away from your soldiers."

I blinked, realizing he meant my team. Cal's team.

"They are not soldiers."

"Sure they are. Different game, different battlefield. Same asshole enemy."

"Get the fuck out, Noah."

"Not gonna happen. Shut up and pass me the tripod." He motioned to what I'd packed up.

"Get it yourself," I snarled, hating myself for taking my anxiety out on this kid. I watched him recreate the situation we had walked away from in silence with our phones, a pen and a few lounge pillows. I wanted him out, but his method got the better of my curiosity. "How old are you, anyway?"

King sat back, eyeing me with a small smile. "Dad tell you which unit I'm attached to?"

"Didn't ask."

"Aren't you the grumpy prick today. Z Unit."

"What?" Startled out of my mood, I stared at him in a new light. Z Unit was a covert op set up in WWII days renowned for being where they shouldn't and doing things that no one else could. It had been disbanded shortly after the war when their talents scared the hell out of a local general. If the kid was part of that unit, then his skills went well above Crossed Rifles. "Well. When the fuck did they resurrect that graveyard?"

"This year. For a group of new ghosts." King ignored me, finishing his set-up. "He didn't look for you. Someone told him where you were, in the car, before he got out. Which meant they had eyes on us and comms on him. Where do you want to start with this clusterfuck?"

I knelt on the floor next to him, working my head around the situation. "You're a spy?" I asked, tracing the route the cars had come from, the little of it that we could see.

"Fuck no. Just your usual paid surveillance in countries we're not supposed to be in. The odd assassination and get-the-fuck-out-of-Dodge damn fast." King sat back, surveying his work. "You think they had a drone?"

"Must've been up damn high. Higher than we could see." I closed my eyes, going back over the few minutes that had mattered. "Joey got out first, all suited up. He was waiting for the hit. On him. Damn, I wish he hadn't seen you the other day."

King shrugged. "Can't go back and change that one. It is what it is. Learn from today, and move forward."

Move forward. I hadn't been thinking beyond today.

King noted my pause with one of his own and looked up, "Liam?"

"Fuck this. Fuck him. I'm getting Selena back from that fucking creeper I put her in with, and we're working this out the way it should go. With everyone."

King rocked back on his heels. "I get to be on the team?"

I snorted at his fake-ass puppy enthusiasm. "Hell, I'll get you pom-poms."

The pressure inside the car could have been cut with a blunt knife. My head ached, my thoughts swirling in a maelstrom of distrust and fury. The latter mostly focussed on myself for slipping so much.
I should have ditched the car.
I should have seen the drone.
I should have taken Selena and run.
Shocks reverberated along my arm as I slammed my open palm on the steering wheel. The jolt did nothing for the soup my brain had become.

"So you didn't take the shot." King stared straight ahead. His feet were propped on my dash, which was quite an accomplishment for a man who had to be over six feet tall. "So what. Maybe you've still got a soul for it."

I was silent for a moment, pushing back line after line of snarky comments and finally settled on a blatant truth. "I'm not sure that counts in our line of work, mate." I stared out over the dashboard, my knuckles a bright white where I clenched them on the steering wheel. I cracked a rare smile. "Besides, souls are overrated."

"I wouldn't know," King stretched out in the passenger seat, reminding me more than ever of a younger Callum Dane.

The thought hurt. Really, truly fucking burned, but I shut the door on it and left it to focus on another day, at the end of all this. If I lived through it, I would have all the time in the world to consider everything I had fucked up in an eternal ten and a half square metre cell.

"You don't get on with your dad?" I asked, selecting what I knew would be most likely to piss him off as my best choice of distraction.

"Family shit," King mumbled, pulling his boots from the dash and tried to stuff them into the small footwell of my sedan.

"We all have that," I grinned; Selena fit there just fine.

"Yeah? I got big shoes to fill," King snorted, "Thigh-high, lace-up, come-fuck-me boots. I've never been able to live up to the old man's name for his actions."

I held back the laugh that wanted to roar out of me.

If nothing else, the kid was a damn fine value. He must fit in well with his unit. Despite his somewhat understandable need to live up to the ghost of a man who fought wars when King was still young enough to think he should idolise his father's efforts.

I tapped out a beat on the steering wheel, considering. "Do you think that you have to?"

King shot me a dark look, his startling blue eyes blazing. "Fix up your own shitbox first, man, before you dive that hooked nose into everyone else's."

Message received.

I nodded, resisting the urge to touch my face, and cast him a quick once over. "Keep giving me bedroom eyes, and we'll have a different problem."

King huffed a laugh, retaining his unimpressed facade, and stared out the window, the tell-tale crook at the corner of his mouth matching my own.

CHAPTER ELEVEN

SELENA

"So you will...have your baby and support your husband who is convicted—" I checked my notes to be sure, unwilling to offend the pregnant woman who sat on the opposite side of my desk, her belly protruding as much as Mila's. The thought of my friend hurt too much, and I focussed on the pages before me. "Ah, not married?" I looked up, making sure I had the right file.

Jesse Wright, male, thirty-one, had killed a man in a drunken brawl. The one-punch hit had ultimately led to the victim's death. Now, I had to deal with the family response to a lost appeal which meant there was a mandatory eight years before a chance of parole. I tried not to stare at the woman in front of me, horrified of the ramifications for her and her baby, as well as the victim and his family.

Trisha Shaw shook her head, patting her belly. "We didn't really have time. We put together an appeal with another solicitor, but it was declined, so now we're working on early parole if that's possible." The woman's sunny disposition shone through tired eyes and sallow skin.

"Okay...so you don't want to lodge another appeal?" I shifted my empty coffee cup, trying to get my head around the family law case Marcus had deposited on my desk.

"No, it took too much energy," Trisha's sunny disposition slipped, her hand over her stomach tightening a little. "We would just like Jesse to see his baby when he arrives."

"That's it?" I asked, scribbling notes frantically, putting out ideas for an appeal in the event Trisha changed her mind. When I received no response, I looked up to see my client with her hand pressed over her bump, and though she looked right at me, her attention was elsewhere.

"He's moving. Would you like to...?" she asked, grabbing my hand before I could argue and tugging me around the desk.

I didn't want to try to extract myself and potentially upset her, so I let her guide my hand over the stretched skin, the surface taut beneath it. If I let her do whatever she had planned, then I could finish up my notes and—

A tiny thing poked my hand.

"I can feel it," I whispered. I stared down at my hand as the tiny being inside the taut skin explored the new touch to its enclosure. "Is that a foot?"

Trisha poked her bump gently. "A hand, I think. That's a foot." She pressed on the other side of her bump, which rocked gently for a moment, then settled as the baby seemed to choose to ignore us.

I stared at her for a too-long moment and made my way back around my desk, sifting papers that had been in the correct order.

"You've never felt a baby kick, have you?" Trisha's voice brought me out of my stupor.

"Hmm? No," I said, with a quick glance up and a smile pasted over my growing terror. Mila had been right there beside me, but I had never tried to touch her or had wanted to. And now, with Liam set on his path— I blinked vapidly at Trisha, recognising that this could be my new future.

"It's a miracle, you know. To have my tiny boy and his father. You might not understand and all but- Jesse. He's such a good man."

"I understand," I smiled my false smile and tried to put some emotion behind my words, but I had become a bare shell of a woman in the face of Trisha's obvious love for her family. "I'll help work out what Jesse needs to do for his parole. See if I can find something to help make sure you get to see each other."

Trisha smiled back, lighting the room up, though my corner of the office remained cold.

My traditional double stack of takeaway coffee cups sat empty on my desk. I kept forgetting, lifting the cold cardboard to my lips, knowing the container was too light, but trying to inhale the dried up dregs nonetheless.

I brushed my hand across my vision, attempting to focus on the screen in front of me, but everything blurred, highlighted by the darkened office.

"Last call before they shut. You know this is a bad habit," Marcus offered, placing fresh cups on my desk and whisking the old ones away.

"You know I love you for it," I yawned and slurped at the coffee. Hot liquid skimmed down my throat, warming me from the inside out. I blinked, and it was like putting high beams on. "Eternally grateful," I sighed, shuffling paperwork as my brain began to function.

"You're amazing." Marcus perched on the corner of my desk, his arms full of law books. He looked like a law student, the nerd in the library. I was certain he must have had as many girls hanging off him as he had throughout our work together.

"We have a business to run. And more cases than just the Logan one." I brushed his name away, hoping I hadn't just jinxed us for the night. The pile of paperwork weighed on my hand.

I had taken on extra cases I normally wouldn't have touched, but doing some smaller, less-intricate cases took up my sleeping hours, which, I had to admit, took up most of my day. And night.

Fortunately, Marcus was as work-obsessed as I was. He wasn't a bad housemate, either. It was one of the reasons we got along.

"Anyone else would be getting drunk at home, but two weeks after he left you, you're still charging on. Admirable." Marcus smiled, apparently under the assumption he had given me glowing praise, and traipsed back to his own desk.

I slipped deeper in my chair, hugging my coffee.

Maybe covering my loss with work wasn't the smartest — or healthiest — cover, but it wasn't just Liam that I missed.

Coffee mornings with Mila, Danny dropping around just to piss Liam off with some new toy he had found the latter couldn't use in his job, Cal...

I had been to the hospital once every few days to sit by Cal's bed. He still hadn't woken, and talking to an innate body seemed odd. When Danny met me at the door to his room, the tears had flowed, and I'd ended up staying while Danny took up the monologue.

So far, Cal had suffered through a blood transfusion, operations that had some...permanent repercussions, and now...the pale figure already looked thinner, more wasted than he had in the years I'd known him, first as Liam's uni mate, then his protege in the police force, and finally as his friend.

The memories of them talking over barbeques, of helping out at Liam's dad's fish shop made me smile. They were more family than friends, and I understood Liam's need for revenge, to take from the man who had stolen years from him.

Sometimes, the smile even broke through the tears as I grieved for them both prematurely.

If I ever got to wrap my arms around Liam again, it would be an utter miracle. But behind the calm that settled over us, I had the feeling that with Cal's survival, we had run through our grace period of those.

Admirable.

Which made Marcus' comment hurt all the more.

"Eat something, please." Marcus placed a bowl of steamed vegetables and tuna on the table. Spicy ginger scents swept over me.

It was becoming his mantra for me. I forced my face into something sociable, relieved when it felt natural.

"Thanks," I smiled wanly, "I'm grateful for anything to take the hospital smell out of my nose."

"Gets stuck there, doesn't it," Marcus said quietly, settling in his chair at my left.

He had taken to sitting beside me rather than across the end of his long, glass-topped table after my first silent meal at his apartment.

Another thing I was grateful for but as terrible as it sounded, even in my own head, I needed space. To process what had happened and what was coming. What was likely to come.

The thought of losing Liam altogether swamped me in a black wave. My spoon dropped from numb fingers and clattered to the table.

"I'm sorry," I whispered, blinking back tears that surfaced far too fast as I fumbled for the spoon.

Marcus covered my hand with his larger one. I studied the dark skin, the soft, perfectly manicured fingers. Not a single callus touched me. The tears flowed faster.

"It's okay, Selena. Here." Marcus rescued my spoon, closing my hand around it with a warm smile. The pity, the knowledge that he knew how this would all end, broke me further.

I placed the spoon in my untouched food and pushed it across to him.

"Thank you, but I'm going to go to bed."

I rose on trembling legs and minced my way along the endless hall to the guest room in dainty steps, willing myself not to fall. Finally, I closed the door of my room, a false barrier between me and the rest of the world.

Then I crumpled onto the plush carpet in a heap and let my grief rage free.

Tiny eyes too big for a scrunched-up, albeit clean, face surveyed me in the review mirror with all the knowledge of his small world.

"Turn left here," Trisha said, holding her belly.

"Are you okay? Tell me if I need to go slower." I gave her a concerned glance, hoping her stitches held. Baby Aiden had made an appearance just after Trisha had visited my office. And despite being told that he shouldn't go anywhere until his vaccinations were up to date, Trisha insisted on taking him to see his father. With no small qualms of our own, Marcus and I had agreed I would drive her to and from the jail and ensure contact with the child was limited to give our best duty of care.

"Oh, I'm fine. I just can't wait for Jesse to hold his little boy for the first time," Trisha laughed, the sound bouncing around the interior of her car.

Aiden gurgled along behind us in his oversized car seat.

I chanced a glance back at the baby, who had managed to stuff both fists into his mouth.

"Talented," I smiled, then it dropped as I considered my next words carefully. "Are you going to be okay– with home or food for you at all?" I bit my lip, hoping the question didn't sound like pity or charity, but I couldn't think of any further ways to phrase it.

Finally, I sighed and leaned back, hyper-aware of every car on the road and every side street that suddenly seemed a threat to everything.

"We're just fine; you don't have to worry about us. My mum gave us some blankets for him, and Jesse's mum has cooked for us, so we have plenty of food." She laughed again, and I relaxed. "And of course, the grandmothers will look after him when I go back to work in six weeks. The doctor said I'd be fine to work again by then."

I blinked at the road, straining my emotional brain to recall that Trisha worked stacking boxes on a night shift at a local department store. "I'm sure you'll be fine," I said automatically, flicking my indicator on and parked in the visitor's space.

"We sure will be." Trisha bustled about, collecting all her baby things, protesting when I added her bags to my own. She collected her baby, and I got us signed through the visitor's books, leaving most of our things with security on the provision that Trisha could come back out to change the baby as needed.

The most time I had been able to secure Trisha was thirty minutes, but that also included Jesse's right to hold his child, as he was formally recognised on the baby's birth certificate.

Trisha pressed Aiden to her shoulder while we waited, her other hand pressed lower, over the site of her emergency caesarean surgery. I shifted my notes in my hand, keen to try to talk Jesse into an appeal.

The doors opened, and Trisha took several steps into the room where a man sat in his prison garb, freshly showered as we had requested for the child's health.

A tall man who reminded me forcibly of Liam ten years ago turned to embrace Trisha, tracing the baby gently in her arms. He looked over at the guard, who nodded, and he stripped the buttons of his shirt open to cradle his newborn son skin-to-skin.

When he looked up at me, his face was glazed with silent tears, but it was joy that I read in his eyes, not anger.

I smiled as best I could, but my lips sat frozen. I clutched my notes and retreated to the far side of the room, giving the couple and their child privacy, though I suspected a circus could have raged on around them, and they wouldn't have taken any notice at all.

The guard motioned to me when our time was nearly up, and I stepped forward, unwilling to break up the scene.

Jesse was the first to look up with baby Aiden squished in a perpetual hug between his parent's bodies.

"Thank you for arranging this. I know it takes effort and...well— Most people don't want anything to do with me. Which is understandable."

"You're welcome," I answered, still trying to gauge this man after his conviction. "It seemed the thing to do." I cringed at my own words, but Jesse smiled.

"You've given me far more than I deserve."

I held up appeal papers behind Trisha's back. "Do you want me to..."

But Jesse shook his head, and I slipped them back into my folder before Trisha could see what I had done.

"More than I deserve." His smile was happy, but Jesse's eyes were sad as he stroked his son's face and bid him goodbye. He caught my gaze one last time. "Thank you." He buttoned his shirt as the guard escorted him away, and I led Trisha back to her car, Aiden content and asleep on her chest.

I pulled the door closed behind me, still tasting salt. The image of Jesse holding his son, Trisha's pride and the peace in his face was etched into my mind. The cool wood of the door pressed to my back as I leaned on it, my hands pressed over my face.

"Hey, good to see you– ah, hell." Marcus thumped across the floor with as little grace as I had ever heard him have. His arms wrapped around me, tugging me away from the door.

"I don't need to be manhandled," I protested weakly and hiccuped a laugh.

"If that's what it does to you, you don't go back there." Marcus passed me a full coffee thermos, pressing me into pillows on the soft lounge. Tears ran down my face as he stroked my back, cooing slightly.

"You're such an old man," I grumbled.

"I am a sexy, wealthy bachelor," Marcus protested. "With a perfect work-life balance. And maybe a grumpy man. But not old. Yet," he added as an afterthought.

"Have you ever thought about getting old?" I asked, swiping across my eyes. My hand came away damp.

Marcus shifted across the two-seater sofa. "Sometimes. I mean, financially, we have the business. And that's strong, despite the time we've spent on the Logan fiasco."

"It is that," I stretched my shoulders, leaning back and bumped Marcus' arm. "Sorry."

"It's fine. I'll keep working, finding new cases until one day, it bores me. Then I'll find something else to do."

"Really?" I sipped from my thermos. "Oh, god. Thank you for this."

"Seeing the family ripped you up?" Marcus stared down at me.

I blinked at his nearness, at the sympathy in his eyes, and the space closed in on me. Twisting around to put a bent knee between us, I realised his arm lay beneath my head and moved that, too.

"If you think that will be me—" I started, my voice shrill and rising in octaves with every word.

"Of course it won't." He smiled, and it was genuine. I sighed, relieved to be off the hook for that one. Marcus' smile twisted. "Thankfully, you don't have children with the man. Is there any chance?" he asked idly, his hand resting on my knee.

I froze, the same petrified inability to make a decision flooding me, though my mind told me to unload the contents of my thermos onto my business partner's fine lawn shirt.

The respectable part of my brain told me I needed to be able to face this man in the morning.

Logan might have screwed with my life, but I'd be damned if he fucked with my business to boot. And besides, I had to defend Liam at the end of the shemozzle he had made of what should have been a very defendable case.

Jesse's peace at holding his son washed over me.

"No wonder you do so well in the courtroom with that level of objectivity." Pressing my hand over my stomach, I rose with more grace than I expected. "There's no chance," I said softly and walked away with a straight spine.

I made it halfway down the hall that led past the entrance foyer when I heard Marcus' answer, just as soft.

"Good."

Closing my eyes, I stood in the shadow of the entrance foyer, breathing. The warmth and scent of Liam swept around me, submerging me in a fast forward reel of memories: meeting him in the coffee shop at uni, falling asleep in class because we had both been up all night, arguing benchmark cases and semantics until we were blue in the face — or red, as we went through Liam's collection of ports.

Mostly him watching me while I studied or poking holes in my arguments. Which hadn't seemed creeper-ish at the time and still didn't though some part of me knew that just maybe, it should. Helping him buy his first house and trying to explain we weren't married when the estate agent gave us a knowing look.

The day I had signed the contract for my own business, trying to resist screaming it to the world, and Liam driving me around the city so I could sing at the top of my lungs in a safe place, without offending anyone. And despite my knowing that I had a horrendous singing voice, Liam never said a word.

Going out in his father's boat, sleeping on the sand, when I knew he was nearby and that I was safe.

I was always safe because he was always there.

And he was always there because he loved me.

The thoughts ran through each other, colliding in a mishmash of memory. I pried open blurry eyes, blinking at the moving shadows on the floor. Tears dripped off the end of my nose, and I knew I must look like an utter and complete mess.

"I'm sorry. That was uncalled for," Marcus said to my right as I studied the moving shadows.

I tilted my head. "It's okay," I answered absently.

"No, really, it's not. I've been alone too long, and you come in and make me realise the changes I would need to make to have a woman permanently in the house."

The shadows moved again, and I decided my tears weren't the cause. Marcus kept rambling away. I ignored him, my eyes tracing the movement to the entry to his apartment, and held up a hand.

Marcus broke off, stuttering until I pointed down.

"Were you expecting anyone?" I asked softly, not taking my eyes off the shadows.

Marcus' silence spoke for itself.

I stared at the door, waiting, and when the knock came, I launched into action, disregarding Marcus' cry of horror behind me. The door handle slipped in my grip. I grabbed at the frame and yanked it open.

Familiar eyes stared back at me, his mouth curving in a rise from boredom to utmost pleasure as I stared back, my heart pounding traitorously.

CHAPTER TWELVE

LIAM

A flurry of dark chocolate curls accosted me at chest height, her lithe frame rocking me back onto my heels.

"You absolute bastard!" Selena shrieked, wrapping her arms around my neck and kissing me solidly. "You never– you didn't—" she cut herself off, staring over my shoulder and slowly descended to hide behind my bodyline. "Who's that?" she whispered into my chest.

I stroked a thumb down the side of her face, blotchy with emotion, though the red that rimmed her eyes told me that her tears had been more recent than our arrival.

"A friend. May we?" I asked, not addressing the movement behind Selena, still drinking her in.

"Of course," she tried to step away from me, gesturing us inside.

I wrapped my arm firmly around her waist, pulling her into me.

Marcus stood at the end of a short hallway, his hands deep in his pockets, his face closed.

"Marcus," I nodded to him.

The middle-aged solicitor nodded once and turned on his heel to disappear into the depths of the apartment.

"Friendly," King snorted behind me.

"Get used to it," I agreed.

Selena looked from me to King and back, studying my clothes. "You boys have had an adventure."

"You could say that," King muttered, closing the door and locking it behind us. "He's not going to come back armed, is he?"

"Only with food and beer." Marcus reappeared on cue, pressing a cold glass bottle into my palm.

I waved it away, needing a clear head for whatever conversation was forthcoming. King took it for me.

Marcus studied the soldier behind me and raised a perfect eyebrow.

Selena giggled into my shoulder as he walked away, her arms wrapped around my ribs in a death grip.

"I've missed you."

"Has he touched you?"

Our words collided, and I settled her more possessively against my side. Selena giggled again, her bloodshot eyes at odds with her broad smile. I leaned down to kiss her lightly, revelling in the warmth of her lips, the way her coffee and chocolate scent coiled around me. She mewled in protest when I drew back a fraction.

"If he has touched you, I'll kill him myself."

Her hesitation was enough to boil my blood.

"It's fine; he hasn't done anything," she reassured me, laughing again.

I stared at her suspiciously.

"He hasn't done anything *yet*," King said behind me.

Selena dissolved into giggles, slipping her hand beneath my arm to shake hands with King.

"I don't know who you are, but you can stay," she whispered, though it was likely loud enough for the next-door neighbour to hear.

"I'm good with that," King caught my eye with a grin, though the straight line of his shoulders belied his tension.

"I needed to see you. And you were right," I gave her a gentle squeeze, dropping a kiss to her head.

"I'm always right," Selena predictably proclaimed. "Wait. What am I right about?"

"Everything." I kissed her again in front of Marcus, just to make the point, and turned to her business partner when I came up for air. "What's going on with the Logan case?"

"Uh, down here, and we dropped it because you said so," Selena poked me, then blinked, facing Marus.

His silence spoke volumes.

"Maybe you're not right all the time," King leaned forward to whisper in her ear.

Selena batted him away, though a smile played across her lips, and my heart ached.

Hell, I've missed that smile.

I'd missed everything about her, from her scent, her taste, the feel of her wrapped around me. And I planned to do a hell of a lot more of that very soon.

"He's not doing a lot that I can tell. Some drug deals. Danny forwarded me files I can send through to you." His gaze flicked to Selena, hesitating, then back to me. "And I still have the judge who will push to take on the trial, should we have the opportunity to go further with the case."

"Appreciate it," I murmured, waiting for the fallout, but when it happened, it wasn't directed at me.

"You asshole," Selena seethed quietly. "If you tell me that you kept this to yourself because of him," she advanced on Marcus, throwing her thumb over her shoulder in my direction, "you might find yourself in an empty office in the morning."

Marcus stared over her shoulder, silently beseeching me for help.

My lips twitched at the thought of letting her go at him — if he actually made a pass at her. But he had been helpful, and if what I planned next came off, I'd need Marcus' help as an outside influence more than ever.

After a long moment, I leaned down to brush my lips over Selena's ear, earning a shiver I wanted her to repeat later when I had more skin exposed.

"He did it for you, not just the case. He certainly didn't do it for me. You were too close and just the tiniest bit predictable, Sweetheart."

King snorted into his beer behind me.

Selena harrumphed, crossing her arms. "I still don't appreciate being left out in the cold." She prodded bare toes into the tops of my combat boots. "This is an interesting change from your elf shoes."

"His fucking what?" King laughed outright behind me.

I grimaced over my shoulder, not wanting to explain the pointy-toed office footwear I donned under duress daily to go into battle with the politicians who resided upstairs from my task force. Especially since Marcus currently wore a matching pair.

"Get your things," I murmured into Selena's hair, stroking my hand along her back.

She turned to me, wide-eyed. "Everything?"

I nodded, and she fled down the hall to our left, disappearing in a flurry of quick steps.

Marcus twitched, staring behind me. "Moving forward with...whatever? Marcus Simmons," he offered his hand past my shoulder.

"Thanks." King plopped his empty beer bottle in it with a grin.

Marcus stared at his hand as it closed around the glass, a slightly distressed look crossing his face.

"Could you email me everything you have so far, please? I'll be around," I waved vaguely at the apartment block, "for a week or so. If we can have everything set up for any time after that, you'll have a closed case."

"That confident?" Marcus raised the same eyebrow as before.

Not on your life.

"Always." I could lie with the best of them and fool a polygraph. Whether Marcus believed me or not was his problem. He certainly wasn't mine any longer.

"Do you still want me to run the case?"

"If you think you can close it."

Marcus nodded his confirmation as Selena reappeared with a small bag slung over her shoulder.

"That's it?" I stared, "I've seen you pack more for a fucking picnic."

Selena sent me a glowing smile that did strange things to my insides.

"That's all. Thank you for your hospitality." She hugged Marcus with one arm.

His hands settled on her waist in a gesture that was far too comfortable for me. "Remember what I said," he looked at me over her head, though he spoke to her, "about families and children." He looked her full in the face.

Selena stood frozen for a minute that strung out for far too long, her chestnut waves cascading almost to her waist.

Had it only been two weeks since I had last held her? So many things seemed to have changed.

Finally, she stepped back from him, pushing away a little.

"I remember," she said, her voice brittle.

Marcus nodded, slipping his hands into his suit pants pockets as we left him in an empty apartment.

Selena sighed as the door closed.

King liberated her small bag, though she didn't fight it, seemingly content to hold her laptop case.

"What was that about?" I asked lightly as we made our way back to the elevator.

Selena shrugged. "He was just being an asshole," she sighed, leaning into me. "I was so tired, and now—"

I let King get a few steps ahead at the elevator bank, where he jabbed at the call button.

"You'd better not be exhausted, Sweetheart," I brushed my lips over her ear, travelling down her neck in a trail of kisses. "I have too much catching up to do with you." Her skin erupted in a flurry of goosebumps, and she rewarded me with a sigh.

I ushered her into the elevator, taking a last glance along the hallway, unsurprised to see the light shining from Marcus's door as he pulled it closed a second time.

"You've been hiding out in an executive highrise in the city centre," Selena completed her circuit of the suite and returned to me. "Are you shitting me? You've never been cliche, Liam."

I snuffed out a laugh, but I couldn't help the smile that played on my lips.

I have her back.

Right now, Logan, Joey and all the rest of his entourage of thugs could go fuck themselves. I had my girl back.

And this time, she would stay mine.

"Actually, we've been hanging out in a dodgy room, sharing a bed together."

I had left King at the bar where he had latched onto the first thing with legs without regard for gender.

"With dirt floors?" Selena raised an eyebrow.

"Hell, I've missed you." I pulled her into my arms, brushing my lips across her temple. I wanted to devour her on the spot, could feel her throbbing against my palms, but first things first.

Her eyes dropped closed, she tilted her head back against my hand. I traced patterns on the base of her skull, earning a small moan I might not have heard if I hadn't been studying her face. But after two weeks apart, I needed to reacquaint myself with every inch of the woman I had taken for granted for nearly two decades.

"It won't happen again," I promised her, crushing her against my chest.

"Sexy, but can't breathe." Selena tapped my arm gently.

I laughed, holding her for one second longer. "Sorry. I just—" the words caught in my throat. I swallowed, staring at her.

"I get it," she murmured, tracing over my face with tentative fingertips. "But Liam— isn't this dangerous? Being together? Isn't this why you left?" she dropped her hand to my chest, pressing over my heart, though her eyes never left mine. "I understand why you did that, too."

"But you were the one who had it right, Sweetheart. We *are* stronger together. I should have listened to you." I smiled, taking the intense edge off my words, though I still didn't answer her question.

"Yes, you bloody well should have," she laughed at me, tugging at my shirt. "Are we alone for a bit?"

"We're good. I haven't called anyone yet. I needed—" I rubbed the back of my neck.

Too soon? I lost myself in those dark chocolate eyes and let the base instinct run free that had been on the back burner for too many years. My mind went back to our uni years, and some later nights I had tried to fill with random females who never made it to the mark Selena set in my head or to sunrise.

She'd had her own flings, but none of those had lasted either, and I had burned every time I saw another touch her.

But her eyes had most often been on me, even when she was with someone else.

"I need you. Time with you," I corrected by habit, straightening.

Selena surveyed me with a dollop of exasperation. "After that– everything, are you fucking kidding me, Liam?" she sighed, then rose onto her toes and kissed me.

My world disappeared into the coffee-caramel taste of her. Soft lips barely contacted mine, and I did a bad job masking my desire to push her further.

A desire I had always put a damper on, unwilling to give in to what we had in case I broke it.

But these few weeks of duress had taught me just how tentative that happiness could be, and be damned if I wouldn't claim it all right now.

CHAPTER THIRTEEN

SELENA

Liam's hands wound around me, tugging at my clothes in a near frantic gesture. And as badly as I would take the quick fuck against the door, more than happy with any contact he gave, if we had time together with everything else going on in our mad-ass world, I would make sure we would also take it slow.

Running my hands over Liam, who was tugging gently at my own clothing, one button at a time, I had the belated thought that I might regret that.

"Slow?" he murmured against my mouth, flicking his tongue over my bottom lip. His hand fisted in my hair, tugging back gently as he wound curls around his fingers.

I nodded, revelling in the feel of him all around me. "I don't want to rush. But you know, don't torture me or anything."

I opened my eyes to find Liam's an inch from mine, his breath kissing my lips. But the look in those eyes was nothing short of wicked. Swallowing hard, I tilted my head back, pressing up onto my toes.

His hands flexed around my waist as his lips contacted mine, his tongue sweeping across sensitive skin, though I would have let him kiss me anyway he liked, without him asking.

It was one of those odd things between us. I knew Liam wouldn't hurt me, and even despite how we had left things when he had pushed me away, I knew that he loved me, at least as much as I did him. Amounts had never mattered, or the petty *I love you more* bullshit I'd experienced as a teen.

Just knowing was enough.

I didn't need proof, but if he was offering, then I sure as hell wasn't going to say no to him.

His kisses seared a path across my lips, along my jawline, as he tipped my head back further with a gentle tug, wrapping my hair around his fist.

I whimpered when he nipped gently at my pulse, fluttering madly beneath my skin, then soothed the brief bite with his tongue.

That simple, short pain took every last remnant of reservation, of fear, with it.

Arching in his hands, I traced my fingers over Liam's shoulders, running across the mass of muscle and scar tissue beneath his shirt. He groaned softly against my throat at the touch.

"I should have pushed you years ago." I sighed as he trailed kisses over my neckline and across the tops of my breasts, following the path of goosebumps that rose over my skin with his tongue. "Why did we wait?"

Liam lifted his head with a groan. "Why? Are you fucking– why do you think?" he demanded in a voice rough with desire. His eyes reflected his intent.

I shrugged, tracing the lines around them that someone else might have called intense but that I simply knew as Liam. "Because you have some intricate sense of honour and duty and a smidge of fear for some stupid reason that you weren't worthy."

Liam stared at me, a slow smile loaded with sinful promise on his lips. "I waited because I love you."

His head dipped, stealing my response, filling my heart with everything I had ever needed and never knew I was missing until that moment.

Liam swept me up into his arms, carrying me into the bedroom and deposited me on the bed in a gentle pile. I didn't argue or fight him. After that, who would? I'd been mad for this man for too many years to count, had tried to ignore the scant few one-night stands he had. Those had hurt like hell; when I knew he didn't see me like that, or maybe he did — but neither of us had acted on it until the first attack Logan had made on our lives.

I shook my head, pushing the bastard away.

I won't let you impinge on my moment with the man I love, you psychotic asshole.

"You okay?" Liam tugged my top down, rolling my nipple between roughened fingertips, the bud already tight and stupidly sensitive.

I gasped, gripping his shoulders tight, and banished every other presence from the room except for Liam. "I'm fine." I tugged at his shirt. "Get this off."

"Demanding, Sweetheart?" Liam paused to take the nipple he tortured between his teeth briefly, and I arched off the bed at the sensations crashing over my body.

"Always," I whimpered, watching as he shucked his shirt over his head, revealing the hardened body he kept punishing long after he left the army. My gaze traced over the ridges of muscle, the carved quality of him I'd known but never been able to appreciate from this angle before. "You're so beautiful," I whispered.

Liam snorted, "I fall well short of that, Sweetheart." He brushed his fingers almost automatically over his side, where the mangled flesh disappeared around his back.

It had healed poorly; he hadn't allowed the medics to bandage or treat him the way he should have been. That refusal gave him a constant reminder of the desert, and I suspected that deep down, he liked it in a twisted way that was all Liam.

"You are to me." I shimmied out of my top, reaching for my skirt as his smile softened, tracing my movement with his gaze.

Liam caught my hands on my skirt, tugging the sides gently. "Let me."

I nodded, my mouth dry as he slid the material down my legs, taking my lace knickers with it. Fumbling at my back, I struggled to work the clip on my bra. Left in just his jeans, Liam grinned, reaching behind me to flick the clasp with one hand.

"And I thought you'd be out of practice," I grumbled, tossing the scrap of material to the end of the bed.

Liam leaned forward, caging me in beneath his arms, his body held taut just above me.

I held back a gasp, every inch of me arching up to him by reflex action, my skin prickling with electric charge where our bodies should have touched but didn't.

"I'm on my game," Liam dipped his head, kissing me hard, deep. "Fuck, I need you."

His words sent a zing of pleasure shooting through me, and this time I didn't hold back from the gasp that rose to my lips. He plunged his tongue between them, his body nestling between my legs to free his hands, cupping them around my face.

I writhed beneath him, the pleasure of having his weight over me pushing the rest of the world away until there was only the two of us left.

Tugging my shirt over my head in a move that should have been awkward, wiggling my shoulders to get out of the thing, but wasn't — maybe because we spent so much time together.

Liam trailed kisses down my throat as he slipped his fingers into the waistband of my skirt, tugging it down my legs to discard it. Roughened fingertips traced along my inner thigh, bare to him, his touch light.

I moaned when he drew circles around my navel with his tongue, his hands and mouth moving closer to where I throbbed and ached. I pressed my palms into the bedding and clenched them as his tongue joined his fingers.

"Dammit, Liam, I'm not supposed to be at this point yet," I choked on a cry as he licked from the sensitive skin he teased — already slick with my desperation and need — to my clit. A raw cry tore from my lips, matching his groan as he stroked his tongue along every inch of exposed flesh.

My world narrowed to his hands wrapped around my thighs to the path his tongue seared over my skin. Teasing with tiny flicks, he sucked my clit between his lips, grazing with gentle teeth, so sweetly that I fell apart in his hands.

Liam kicked his jeans free and slid along my body, a fine sheen of sweat aiding his path.

"Wait," I protested, struggling to open my eyes, the room swirling around me as I tried to focus on him. "I wanted to—"

"You'll get to," he murmured, catching my hand in his to lick at my fingertips.

I watched his mouth close around my fingers, a shiver working its way along my body. "You have to stop. I can't cope with this much attention after so long," I whispered, letting him draw me into his embrace.

"Can't you?" he kissed me lightly, slowly, sending my head whirling. He drew my hand down, wrapping my fingers around his thick cock.

My eyes flew open, a tiny mewl dying a messy death in my throat. "I want—" I whispered, finding how my hand fit around him — barely — and what he liked...quickly.

I've barely touched him, and my mouth is watering.

Visions of his body arched over mine, his tongue discovering every secret of my body hurtled through me. It might have felt slutty with another man, but it didn't with Liam. I wriggled, sliding down his body but his arm around my waist held tight, trapping my hand around him between us.

"Not yet, Sweetheart," his arm released me. Checking that I wasn't going to wriggle away from him, Liam slipped his fingers between my legs, sliding them through my arousal mixed with his saliva. "You're dripping," his words were laced with a smirk I couldn't see, my mouth pressed to his, though heat rushed to my cheeks. "Let's see how long you last this time."

My gaze flew to his, my fingers still stroking him languidly. "This time?"

Liam nodded with that sinful smile, sliding two fingers deep into me.

A moan tore from my lips. I arched back as he found a place inside me that had been waiting for him.

"Stroke me while I make you come again," he murmured against my lips, sliding his tongue into my mouth as he kissed me deeply.

I traced my fingers around his girth, then length, getting used to the feel of him.

"You're going to break me," I whimpered, meaning it in more than one way. "Tell me this isn't why you waited."

I was torn between desperate for him inside me and terrified at the same time. His thumb brushed my clit, and I tightened around him, aware of every ridge of his fingers, every scar as he drove them deeper into me.

"I'll be careful with you," Liam tugged me closer, nestling me against his shoulder as his fingers quickened.

Breath shuddered between my lips as I tried to remember to stroke him, but the pleasure that bombarded me was too much to concentrate on anything but the scent of our arousal that whirled around me in a maelstrom of our own making.

CHAPTER FOURTEEN

LIAM

I love you.

She screamed the words at the height of her climax. Her tentative, distracted strokes as I toppled her over the edge of her pleasure almost took me with her.

Long formed restraint held me back from taking her then, but only just.

She clenched around my fingers in a series of aftershocks, accompanied by tiny moans. I pulled her tighter into me, every inch of her pressed skin-on-skin in a new realm of pleasure all of its own.

I love you.

Damn, I'd been an idiot to wait, but maybe it had given us this incredible moment that I would have given another decade to have if I knew it was the promised prize at the end.

The woman I adored to the depths of my soul curled around me, her limbs soft with pleasure. The scent of her coated my skin, sinking deep into me to where she had always been.

I stroked my fingers along her arm, trailing the side of the marred flesh where I knew sensation returned. Selena shivered in a slow, lazy motion that stirred every part of me.

"You're incredible," she murmured, raising heavy lashes to stare up at me. "Honestly. I can't– I don't want to imagine a day or night without you in it." Her smile was completely guileless while my stomach dropped out from beneath us.

I covered it with a slow kiss that earned another moan, pushing the earth-shattering thought to the background. "Sweetheart, we haven't started yet." I slid my fingers over her stomach, tracing the lines of lean muscle there, over the soft flare of her hip.

Her fingers wrapped around my wrist. "You can't be serious. I've just– no, Liam. I can't," her eyes widened as I traced over the sensitive flesh, still coated in her arousal.

I held her gaze, bringing her to that tip of pleasure, again and again, only to let it drop back.

"I can't," she panted in my arms. Something wild grew in her gaze, her back arching as I slid two fingers inside her, brushing over her clit with the heel of my hand. Her breath came in short gasps, and I bent my head to swallow them.

Her lips tasted sweeter as she twisted beneath me. I pinned her with one hand to her stomach, working the other in an increasing rhythm.

"You will," I promised, kissing her again as she broke, crying out into my mouth. I wrapped my arms around her, sliding my knee between her thighs, adding a little pressure to keep her high for a little longer. Finally, her breathing

136

settled. "Sweetheart," I coaxed her eyes open with feather lips kisses across her lips, "do you still have—"

"Huh? Oh, yes." Selena wiggled an arm free, rolling it over to show the tiny dot where her implant had gone in.

I grinned, remembering the day she'd had it put in, holding her hand while she gripped it fiercely. I had taken her out for ice cream afterwards, though I always suspected she'd sulked for far longer than was necessary to draw extra sympathy.

"Do you mind if I don't use..." I slipped my fingers from inside her, coating myself with her arousal.

She followed my motion with her gaze, nodding jerkily. "Please," she whimpered, her fingers wrapped around me, stroking in a building rhythm as I settled between her legs.

"Easy, sweetheart," I murmured, tugging her hand free to a string of protesting mewls. "I won't last long if you keep that up."

"Oh," Selena whispered, her eyes wide. I pressed against her entrance, sliding inside her easily from the pleasure I'd given her earlier. "Oh," she whimpered again, wrapping her knees up around my waist, wriggling beneath me. Her moans tumbled around me, but then there had only ever really been her for me.

My control was on a tight leash. Who knew how many nights I'd fallen asleep, fantasising about just this, taking pleasure only in the shadows, but never with her. The college boy's dream.

"Christ, Selena," I growled, gripping her shoulders gently, careful not to hurt her. "You feel—"

She moved her hips, pushing up on me, so I sank into her in a smooth moment, and I lost the ability to think.

I clenched my hand around her hip, stroking her hip bone with the pad of my thumb, and she let out a guttural moan to match mine.

It might have been the sexiest thing I had ever heard.

Drawing back, I caught her gaze, losing myself in those luminous, chocolate eyes. Her body moved with mine perfectly, the way I had always imagined, as though she preempted every movement. Sweat rolled between her breasts; I traced a path back to her throat with my tongue, revelling in the taste of her, the feel of her around me.

Her body tightened, and I increased my pace, pushing her over the edge and holding her there. I drew every last cry from her lips until my control frayed, and I tumbled with her into a world of our own making.

Selena's chest rose with mine as she sprawled across my body. Sunlight from the open windows filtered into the room, covering her with a blanket of warm, white light. She moved gently over me, our skin slick with sweat and sated need.

Selena propped herself up on her forearms, staring at me with sleepy eyes and a smile that made me want to roll her over and have her again. If I had the energy.

"I love you," she whispered, the words brushing over my lips.

I closed my eyes for a moment, drinking her warmth in, savouring it somewhere deep that no one could steal from me. Cupping the back of her head, I twirled luscious curls around my fingers and kissed her fiercely, working for one of those soft moans I loved earning from her.

When she finally gave me one, I tugged her back to my chest, cradling her there.

"Sleep."

After so many sleepless nights, so many hours without her, having Selena in my arms and wrapped around me, I let the exhaustion settle in. Soul deep, the simple pleasure of having the woman I'd always adored finally with me, my mind sank, and I finally managed to rest.

A sharp rap brought me out of my cloud of pleasure, my phone buzzing at the same time. I shifted, watching as Selena woke, her eyes soft and dozy, and fuck me, sexy as hell.

I leaned down to kiss her again, slowly reacquainting myself with every inch of her that I had burned into me but needed the refresher, anyway.

The knock came again.

"Are you going to get that?" Selena asked, stretching against my chest.

I shook my head, stroking my hand along her arm, tracing the puckered skin there and felt the rage rise. Pushing it down took effort and another kiss. Or so I told myself as the rapping became shouts outside the door.

"Get dressed," I advised, backing off the bed with a sigh and pulling jeans on to answer the door.

Danny hung off the doorway and surveyed me with a smirk. "Well, thank fucking Christ for that." He pushed past me, leaving me with a bottle of red in my hands with a hard gaze. "Mandy was found discarded in a dumpster outside where Cal first met her. Where I had to fight for him." The corners of his mouth turned down, an expression unsuited to him as he shoved something into my hands. His expression lightened in an instant, though I knew it was an act, "I think that's the one she likes," he tossed over his shoulder, swaggering into the suite.

"Found these assholes downstairs, milling about like sheep," King grinned. "Thought the brute squad might be looking for you."

"Thanks," I said dryly. "Glad to have you back."

Danny flicked the bird over his shoulder at the room.

"I'm sure he'll grow up one day. But he's right." Black shook his head, slicking his hair back from his face and passed me a bag of plastic containers that were heavy as hell. "Jenny cooked curry."

"Bless." I turned to see Selena in a knee-length blue and white striped shift looking for all the world like she had been working in the office all day, not fucked eleven ways from Friday half an hour earlier.

Bulging biceps engulfed me — and not many people could actually achieve that on me, but Micah managed with ease.

"Good to see you." I pressed a hand to his shoulder. "How are they?" I didn't ask about him, knowing I would get his standard shrug and easy smile despite what turmoil might lie beneath the calm facade.

"They're okay. Worried, of course," his voice dipped, "but coping. They're busy."

I grinned. "What a healthy stress management system we have in place." I shifted back to let Micah in and locked the door behind him.

"Food first," Selena stated as she collected the curry and coffee from Black, kissing the rough man's cheek. She patted his beard lightly, and I growled. "I don't know how Jenny deals with this," she murmured, her brow twisted in consternation.

"With pleasure, babe." Black hugged her until she squeaked and looked over her shoulder at me with a wink. "Take notes, eh?"

I ran my hand over my own smooth face.

"Old habits and new dogs. Or something," Danny laughed.

Minutes later, bowls that had been full were empty in a clutter on the coffee table. Five big men were squashed into sofas that would have struggled to hold four regular people. Selena curled on my lap. She tried to sit on the floor, but the thought of being near her and not touching her broke something inside me that wasn't fixed yet.

As she snuggled against my chest, I knew having her with me would heal those cracks that had threatened me for so long, and she had been the one filling them with putty to keep me from falling apart.

Selena pressed into my chest, winding her fingers through mine as we began to nut out ideas. King listened, and I could see the cogs turning over in his head as he inhaled everyone's input.

When silence fell, he tossed out a few tentative ideas, and I could see the plan forming in it as he talked, letting everyone have their say as the newcomer in the group. The outsider.

But with the skills the boy had in managing unknowns who had worked together in extreme conditions for years, he should have enrolled in officer school, not enlisted as a grunt.

It might be something I suggested to him at the end of all this.

Slowly, their ideas became workable concepts that morphed into tasks, picking out their specialised area as we had always done. Bouncing ideas and playing devil's advocate, King unconsciously fell into the missing role Cal usually provided.

It would be dangerous as hell, and I hated that so much was outside of my control.

But at least this time, we did it as a unit.

CHAPTER FIFTEEN

SELENA

The apartment was silent without the boys in it. Even King had headed down to the bar, all of them promising they would leave the building in different directions and in different cars than they had arrived in. Fortunately, the hotel sat beside a rental car depot with an underground garage that we utilised to maximum effectiveness.

Danny organised transport under a created company name he resurrected from a case unrelated to Logan. Theoretically, the cover company would provide an existing platform to hide behind. It wouldn't stand up to an intensely detailed study, but then, the person prying needed to know where to look for it too.

No matter where I turned, the man haunted me with every step. Which brought me back to the man doing push-ups on the carpet beside me, his body covered in the fine sheen of sweat that popped out the moment he began to exercise. I followed the beads as they gathered in the hollows of hardened, carved muscle, though the scarred section at his side remained clean.

I lay on my back, stretching lightly after my own brief workout, and relished the strain on tense muscles, the stress gathered around my neck. I let gravity tug my body into its usual form with yoga flows that came as an automaton after practising for so many years. "You know you guilted me into this after not providing coffee."

"Hell, you are a demanding little wench, aren't you? I had no idea how the tables would turn once you were mine." Sweat beaded across Liam's shoulders and neck in his customary black singlet, but his words filled me with a warmth that had nothing to do with the heat of the sweating man beside me.

Well, sort of.

I stared at the ceiling, letting that word roll around in my head for a moment.

Mine.

He had certainly taken his time getting around to it, though I hadn't pushed, either. But I was learning.

I studied the decorative architraves above my head. "Marcus provided me with coffee. Several times a day."

Liam paused mid pushup, bracing halfway to the floor. After a moment, he resumed his workout. "Did he."

"Mmhm." I nodded, stretching my other leg over my head and relishing the strain. No part of me regretted asking Liam to take it slow, but if he put me through my paces later on, I might be stumbling around for the better part of a day in recovery. "*Several* times a day," I emphasised the first word.

Liam looked sideways at me. "Are we using coffee as a euphemism for sex? Because as much as I respect the guy, any chance of friendship is out the window if he's touched you." His words were light, but his tone was dark.

A shiver worked its way up my arms, travelling to my core. "No, no one else has touched me, not since I saw you last. Not for a long while, actually," I turned my head away from him and got an eyeful of sunlight. "Argh."

Movement beside me drew my attention back to Liam, but my retina burn whited everything out. His weight settled over me, his hands cupping my cheeks before he kissed me. Soft lips turned hard as his mouth devoured me, every pent up emotion drawn to the surface at last.

"No one else touches you like this. Ever," Liam kissed me again, his lips lingering as his eyes darkened. "You're mine now, dammit. I should have done this years ago."

"Yes, you should have," I replied tartly, smiling into his fathomless eyes, "and yes, I am."

"You are what?" His expression was guarded, reminding me how fragile the ego of this hard man was.

"I'm yours." I drew him down to me, returning his kisses until I forgot where we were and that the blinds were open as he peeled my sweaty workout clothes away.

Liam tasted every inch of my skin, kissing and sucking until the lightest sensation drove me mad. I panted beneath him, scratching my nails along his arms when he teased my breasts, crying out when he used those clever fingers again.

Until finally, I couldn't actually take his teasing anymore and pushed him away.

Liam rolled onto his back on the carpet, lacing his hands behind his head with a bemused grin. His mouth opened, but I held up a finger.

"If you tell me I'm a demanding wench once more, I'll show you exactly how demanding I can be, and it won't involve anything fun," I warned. I kneeled between his legs and slid my hands over the front of his shorts, over the ridge of him that hardened further under my touch. I peeled the material down, holding his gaze, and slid my tongue along the length of his cock.

Liam closed his mouth.

His hand fell to the back of my head, just cupping there, not pushing me down as I discovered every solid inch of him — and there were plenty of those to play with. He swelled between my lips as I learned what he loved most. Just as I had worked him out, Liam slipped his hands beneath my shoulders, drawing me up the length of him as he kicked his shorts free, tossing his shirt next to them.

Sliding my legs over his, I straddled him. Watching his gaze brush over my body was like a physical caress. I shivered, sliding myself the length of him, coating us both with my arousal.

Liam groaned, fisting himself gently in time with my movements, his thumb flicking over my clit. "Don't come. Not yet," he murmured. "I want to feel you tighten around me when I'm inside you."

My breath catching, I nodded, unable to speak with his touch. He moved his hips just enough to slide inside me. Short pants tumbled from my lips as Liam caught my hands, lacing our fingers over my hips. He pushed down hard, pinning me to him as he thrust upward.

My screams ricocheted around the room, both of us moving together in a sea of whimpers and moans that filled my ears until my body tightened around his. I squeezed my thighs to his sides, but he held me impaled by him, pleasure sweeping over me in an endless bombardment.

Shivering, I sank to his chest, boneless.

Liam swept damp hair back from my face, holding me to his chest. "My god, you're beautiful," he said hoarsely.

"You too," I murmured sleepily.

A deep rumble reverberated beneath my cheek. Light fingers traced reverently over my head like I was something special, something different, but I was too tired, too happy to care as sleep tempted me, and I snuggled into his chest.

"You seem to keep thinking we're done," Liam murmured, pressing me into the hardness of him that was not yet satisfied. He drew my chin up with his knuckle to kiss me gently. "And we're nowhere near that, Sweetheart." His eyes glowed with sinful purpose, stealing my breath and my heartbeat.

"I need the memories," I murmured, not thinking, and his eyes took on a different type of glow.

Liam hooked his leg behind my ankle, his arms sweeping down my back. My body yielded to him as he rolled us, and I soaked up the simple pleasure of his body pressed fully against mine. I arched up, Liam bearing down on me, his eyes an intense slate grey that told me he would take what he wanted.

"Keep the memories close," he murmured, grazing his lips over my skin in a path that burned long after he moved away.

His hand curved around my hip, sliding his fingers around my ass, and I had never felt so small or delicate.

Beneath the power of muscle and determination that was all Liam, packaged into the man I loved for so many years, I was okay with that.

His hips flexed, he gauged the way my body arched into him, his hands finding tight purchase as he moved within me. His eyes pierced me as he brought me to the edge of pleasure, again and again, catching me each time I fell.

"Do you forgive me for abandoning you yet?" Liam murmured into my hair.

We laid on the carpet in the sunlight. He traced patterns over my stomach while I rediscovered every scar he possessed. It felt different from this point of view. Not from beneath him; over the years, we had fallen asleep together too many times to count. But from the perspective of being his lover.

The word sat heavy in my stomach, but it was a pleasant pressure, similar to the weight of him over me an hour ago.

And I was still too sated to move.

"I never blamed you. You were a bit of an asshole about it, though," I pointed out, tracing around a cluster of three puckered scars that grazed his ribs. "Which ones hurt most?"

"The asshole is natural." Liam paused while I poked each bullet scar with tentative fingers. "Don't be hesitant. Not you, please," he almost begged but restrained it a little. "You've seen the worst of me."

"And the best of you." I pressed my palms to his cheeks, sliding them to the mangled flesh at his side.

Liam said nothing for a long moment. "I think the worst hurt comes from inside, from who I lost. Not the wounds. The residual pain is...cathartic." His eyes searched mine for understanding.

"I know," I whispered, and having missed him, having thought I had lost him forever, would see him next in prison pyjamas, had nearly crippled me. "Are we going to survive this?" I searched his eyes for a promise no one could give me, least of all the man who was the catalyst of it.

"I want to promise you the moon. But...I know how that one turns out. With dust mingled with blood and a nice note to someone I don't know, pretending I can reconcile their grief when I don't understand my own."

Liam always suffered most from a fear that his failures had cost his team everything, and now it had the potential to happen again. But taking that pain of his temporary loss and throwing it into some sort of work gave me a new appreciation of how he had existed for the past twenty-odd years, battling to push the imposter syndrome back and keep the survivor's guilt at bay.

"You've been there through every black moment, through every night I've struggled to not add another bullet to the collection. Until these last weeks," the hoarse quality returned to his voice.

My hand stilled on the words of the scars, lingering over the mass of destroyed flesh, and external manifestation of the matching chaos I suspected — had always suspected — lay inside him.

"While you were away, I took on a new case — something different." I inhaled, recalling Jesse's expression when he held his son, and the loss of something I didn't understand threatened to overwhelm me.

Liam's arm slipped around my shoulder. "Keeping busy?" he asked lightly, though I knew he said it as a distraction more than anything else.

"It was a family case."

"You don't usually do those." Liam's fingers twined around mine, stroking his fingers over the back of my hand. "Those result in heartbreak. Usually yours," he added.

I winced. "I know, and maybe...that's why I took it up. Because I missed you, or something stupid."

"It's not stupid to miss someone you love." His arms wound around me, tugging me back against his chest.

"That's true," I hedged, "but I didn't have you here with me and...my head wasn't a good place to be right then," I mumbled the words into his shoulder.

Liam laughed, the sound rumbling inside his chest. "Have you seen me?" His smile faded as he tipped my head back so he could stare into his eyes. "Tell me."

Everything about the case came tumbling out: Trisha sitting pregnant in my office, talking about the man she adored despite his being a convicted felon behind bars. Driving into the prison with a baby strapped in her backseat, terrified of every vehicle and sidestreet that suddenly became death traps.

Watching Jesse's moment of peace as he held his child for the first time and the woman who adored him, despite what had happened. That she stood by him. And that he was grateful.

Liam sat silently while I spoke, tracing patterns around my wrists with gentle fingers. When I finished, he picked up my hand, kissing each knuckle.

"And you think this might be what happens to us?" he asked, his breath brushing against my skin.

I gripped his fingers with the trusting desperation of a newborn, my heart aching in my chest, and nodded.

"I thought of how lucky she was to have a baby that would remind her of him every moment he wasn't there. Waking, or otherwise."

"There would be a lot of those moments," Liam agreed with a wry grin, "not that I doubt you, but raising a young child with your man in prison wouldn't be an easy route to take," his eyes held a warning.

I ignored it. "She loved him, despite what happened. What he did," I whispered, and the tears tumbled free, trailing pitifully down my cheeks.

"Hey." Liam brushed my tears away but only succeeded in making a bigger mess. I choked on part of a laugh. "Love is a huge thing. It's why I've been too chicken shit to tell you for so long. It's not fragile, and it's a dark pit of emotion I'm fairly sure no one really understands the depth of, whether you've got your big boy panties on or not."

"There should be a stack of law books on that," I snuffled against my hand.

"Oh hell," Liam laughed, the sound filling the room. "Can you imagine that? How many books?" He spread his arms wide. "It would take up buildings. But seriously, I've seen families do it, soldiers. The baby thing," he paused, pensive.

"It's okay, you don't have to—"

Liam waved me down. "No, I want to. What you've described with Trisha and Jesse. There's a tinge of desperation in the few days between when soldiers get their deployment orders and when they ship out, not knowing if they're going to come back. There's a lot of babies nine months later. Some of the boys get back to see the birth; others don't. Often, the family isn't there for them when they come home."

"It's such a tough time. Desperation doesn't breed good things," I murmured.

I'd seen that enough with clients I had defended, had seen them sabotage their own lives in the few short weeks before a sentence was handed down.

"There's plenty of messy breakups when soldiers are away." Liam's lip curled. "Most couldn't keep it in their pants long enough and focussed on menial problems instead of surviving. It happens on both sides of the line, and it has nothing to do with the enemy we're meant to be fighting. Damn long string of broken hearts."

"Did you have girls throwing themselves at you?" I asked, tilting my head back to look at him, "lonely women who wanted another soldier?" I grinned.

Liam shook his head with the hint of a smile in reminiscence. "More times than you'd think." His smile faded to be replaced by something heavier. "But telling those same women their soldier wouldn't be coming home opened a whole new set of floodgates, and I could never show any emotion."

I frowned. "You weren't allowed to show compassion?"

"Compassion got to be beyond me, after a time. My ghosts followed me about with every visit, adding a new one each time. There are some black moments in there," he said, tapping the side of his head with a wry grin I knew he didn't feel.

I placed my hand over his heart, soothed by its regular beat. "Your black moments make the rest of our issues look pissy," I smiled softly, running my hand over the bristles on his face.

"I'm not blaming you. I'm the fucking idiot who walked away." His kiss sent fire to my heart, despite his harsh words. Liam ran a hand over his head. "And I've been building that stupid boat to occupy time that should have been spent with my hands wrapped around you. *All* of me wrapped around you," he growled, and this time, there was a playful edge to it.

He dipped his head to catch my lips, his fingers tangled in my hair as he demonstrated just how well his body could wrap around me.

CHAPTER SIXTEEN

LIAM

"Eyes?" I asked, scanning the sky, but the drone was too high to pick out anything amongst the clouds.

"Two points to your left and straight on till morning," King muttered, zooming in on his screen. A frown creased golden features beneath freshly shorn hair he'd done himself.

"Fuck off," I grinned.

"There's that vocabulary."

King had fast become a permanent attachment to our crew. I just hoped he would be able to extract himself when it came time.

Every man working with me knew the risks of our actions and was prepared to take them. And Jimmy. The green-haired engineer was our plus one who refused to leave. And with her technical expertise, she bridged the small gap between Micah and Danny's knowledge.

"Hell, no, he's that grumpy bastard pirate who battles the crocodile." Danny tossed over Micah's shoulder.

The big man rolled his eyes. "Alligator." Micah shook his head. "Didn't your Mumma tell you the right fairy tales?"

"I'd make comments about your Mumma, but she feeds me. So, I'm not game."

"Please tell me Laura can cook. ' Cause you sure as fuck can't," Micah feigned horror.

"Baby, she has half the city cooking there. She doesn't need it."

"More for us, and here," Jimmy poked her head out from behind her screen, flicking her fingers toward the TV screen that took up half the wall, in a magician's wave, "three, two one—" she closed her fist.
The screen King and I hunched over, squiggled sideways with static and went blank.

"What the fuck?" the younger man muttered.

I frowned, but a giggle across the room raised my head.

Jimmy flicked a middle finger at the TV screen against the wall, where the drone blew up to ten times its size. I grinned as that same finger rubbed her nose, aimed at me as I was tackled from behind by a body that clutched me with need and love. "Danny, that better as fuck not be you," I snarked, not looking at him, knowing he was across the room.

More than one bird flew free.

"Admit it; you like having them back."

I spun in her arms, catching Selena against me. "I sure as fuck love having you back," I kissed her, ignoring the catcalls behind me.

"Mmh. But I have to go, don't I?" Selena watched me with those deep eyes I'd fallen into too many times and now never wanted to extract myself from.

"You want to battle with Mr Fucking Psychopath, be my guest. I'll stand behind you with something big." Danny yelled.

Micah smiled over his head, shaking his head woefully. "Nothing big enough there, my friend," he murmured, just loud enough for the room to hear.

King broke the silence with a belly laugh that set Black off, and the two hard bastards rolled about on the floor like kindergarteners.

"When you're fucking right," I muttered, pinning King with a glare that he pointedly ignored. "And as for you—" I kissed Selena soundly, holding her to my chest so I could feel her heartbeat in time with mine. "You are going back to Marcus." I leaned forward to whisper in her ear, "Though I'll enjoy seeing you rip Logan to shreds in the courtroom."

Selena laughed against my lips, drawing back just enough to see my eyes. "I won't get the chance to if you're facing off with him."

She owned me in front of the room, and I didn't care, though I kept watching her. I smiled slowly at her. "You're okay with this, Sweetheart?"

She shivered, a reaction I knew came now when I called her that. "Whatever you need." She feigned indifference, but I could see straight through it.

I pressed my lips to her ear, tangling my fingers in her hair. "Sweetheart, I will never have you around that man. If he tries to hurt you, he will never get the chance before any of us get to him." I moved back for her to see the shield wall of men who would sacrifice themselves between her and Logan.

156

Selena stared at them all with wide eyes.

"You guys are all assholes," she muttered, clutching the giant coffee King passed her.

The boy was a quick learner. I gave him a sideways grin, still focussed on Selena. She was my only focus whenever she was in the room.

"Hmm," Selena watched me over the rim of her coffee as she raised the travel mug and closed her eyes in bliss. "You can stay," she murmured.

I cracked a thin smile, still thinking of Logan. "Gee, thanks," I said softly, watching those chocolate eyes close with the utmost pleasure.

Selena snorted, her dark lashes flying open. "I meant him," she waved at King, who grinned back.

When I turned to him, his gaze raked me insolently.

"That's why you're not an officer?" I let my gaze settle into the cold, hard facade that had kept many a youthful soldier in line.

His bright blue eyes shuttered under my stare. "That, and some other reasons."

Danny met my eyes over King's hunched form as the young soldier studied the screen in front of him, pointing out weaknesses.

I didn't know whether I should kick him out of the apartment or offer him a job.

The boys packed up their gear in silence. Each would go their own way, take their own path to achieve the end result: Wayde Logan would no longer be a threat to anyone. Not to our families and not to anyone else's.

I was under no illusions that otherwise, once the madman was done with us, he would continue to terrorise others.

The difference was that this time, we did it together.

Danny nodded to me, his hand on Micah's shoulder as they left the apartment. King leaned against the far wall. He made contact with each man once, and it was more than enough to secure his place within the team.

He had our backs, and we had his, if this thing went sideways. Which there was a damn fine chance of happening.

Black gripped my shoulder too hard.

"You stay out, no matter what." I held the man's onyx gaze. He might have the years on me, but my experience was more than a match for his.

His lips twitched. "If you say so, boss." He added a twang to the end of his words.

I snorted; he'd turn up at some point, regardless of what I told him to do.

"Just keep those girls safe." My throat constricted on the words.

Black held my gaze, not looking away, and I was glad to have him watching over the heart of our family.

"I'll bring you a box of glitter after this is all done," he grunted. "Ashley's got the shit everywhere."

"Ah, you can be our sparkling knight, come to our rescue," I grinned, nodding to the door as it closed behind Micah and Danny, Jimmy trailing between them. "Get outta here."

Black snorted. He looked up, his gaze lingering over my shoulder. His lip curled in a familiar sneer, and I didn't have to look behind me to know that King had flipped him off.

The door closed behind the last of my original team, leaving us in a sinking silence that permeated my skin. Finally, I turned on my heel to face the remaining occupants of the room. The necessary detachment sank into me, an automatic response in the face of battle.

It might not be the desert, but this was no different in terms of the man we faced off against. I just hoped that when Selena realised how cold I could be, it didn't send her running as far from me as those sexy legs would travel.

Her arms wrapped around herself in her usual long-sleeved, black top, the v-neck travelling down her chest to show the swell of her breasts. Paired with her standard dark blue jeans and heels, she was absolutely breath-taking, though I wasn't used to seeing her so uncertain.

Something about her brought out a dark, jealous beast that lived within me — had always done, around her. But now that I'd let its reins go, the beast wanted to destroy anything that endangered her.

Which really put Logan in a whole new world of hurt.

King lounged against the wall like he walked into a battlefield everyday. One leg propped against the wall behind him, a bored look on his face.

I gathered Selena into a tight hug. She didn't protest, just pressed every inch of her harder against me.

"You two have a room for that, you know." King didn't look at us.

I raised an eyebrow. "Practicing your best hooker stance there?" I refrained from using the *son* that dangled at the tip of my tongue, despite that he was young enough for it.

"If it's what works best." King flashed me a smile that might have been cute if it wasn't for the dead eyes above it that reflected my own.

"I'll put you on the corner when we get back then." I paused long enough for his huff to fade into silence, looking down at Selena. Her fingernails dug into my back, but I would take any measure of pain to keep her safe.

She sighed softly, tipping her head back. "I'll stay with Marcus," she murmured. "You need to do...whatever this is." I watched her attempt to swallow, the tears that filled her eyes that she blinked away.

I'll never see you again. Not the way we are now.

The unspoken words hung between us, but after so many years together, living together, and now having her in my arms, she didn't need to say them.

I gripped Selena's arm, pulling her against me. A low growl burned my throat at the thought of her living with another man, even if I knew it was the only way this could play out for her to be safe. "We don't have to do that."

I don't want you near another man.

"Yes, we do." She leaned up to kiss me, her brown eyes igniting something primal deep within me. "Because I need to be able to get you all out of the mess you're currently in. And by all of you, I mean you, Liam, because you won't let anyone else fall for this," she said tartly.

Laughter skittered through the room, my growl dying with it.

King met my eyes over Selena's head. "She's a keeper, mate. If you have one to spare, I'll take her."

I wound my arms around Selena's lithe frame, tugging her to me for what could be the final time. "There's only one woman like her."

Selena smiled into my chest, gripping me with tight fingers painfully over the scar tissue, and I revelled in the sensations she brought back to me.

King nodded, his once-expressive eyes closing down to something cold and soulless.

As much as I had grown to care for the young soldier, I wouldn't want to be on the other end of those eyes if they were directed at me.

It was like looking in a mirror.

CHAPTER SEVENTEEN

SELENA

Liam's fingers burned a path across my lower back as we walked the short distance from the elevator to Marcus' door. He'd pulled the material up as soon as we were out of the car, pressing his roughened fingers against my skin, holding me close.

I breathed sharply, sucking back the tears that threatened to overflow. I wanted these moments with Liam to be a clear memory, not one blurred by my own private pity party.

Liam passed me my usual double stack of takeaway cups as he rapped on the door, tugging my chin up with a knuckle beneath it in a fluid motion. His lips brushed mine once again before they settled against my skin. I opened my lips, letting him taste me as I drew every inch of the memory out. The feel of him, the coffee and spice scent of him, wrapped around me like a shield against what was coming.

The door creaked open — a 'custom' creak Marcus left so he could tell if someone was breaking in or not. Which I had always thought was a ridiculous thing to bother with until my own townhouse was broken into. I shivered at the thought, and Liam's hand on my back tightened possessively. That sent another shiver coursing over me — one that had nothing to do with the terror that I had faced then and everything to do with the man wrapped around me.

I didn't want him to leave.

Marcus coughed pointedly, far too close for my comfort. I pressed deeper into Liam's chest, welcoming that deep growl I was becoming accustomed to.

"Be safe. Please. Come back to me," I whispered, the tears finally running over.

Liam stared into me, deep inside, like he was trying to take me with him. "I love you," he murmured into my hair, pulling me tight against his chest.

I held my coffee out with a squark. "There'll be hell to pay if you spill these," I threatened.

"Damn girl, that's his problem, now." Liam's humour left his face as quickly as it had come on. "I'll see you soon, Sweetheart."

I nodded, closing my mouth as heat rushed up to my cheeks, tears overflowing in an instant.

His searing touch left my back, placing it with an icy emptiness.

Marcus' arm slipped around my shoulder, a poor replacement, turning me into the hall with a few murmured words I heard, but couldn't comprehend. He patted my shoulder in his familiar gesture and straightened my top where Liam's hand had been.

I felt the loss of him even more keenly and turned to look back to find him staring at Marcus with death written across his gaze.

Liam caught the motion, his eyes flickering, returning to their usual warmth before he cast a quick look at Marcus and strode to the elevator bank and out of my sight.

I worked silently on my laptop. A disjointed need to finish tasks that meant little filled me, to close off cases and answer the four hundred and something emails that cluttered my inbox. Anything to keep my mind occupied so my conscience could spend its waking hours waiting for the inevitable phone call. My sleeping hours, though few, were taken up with increasingly horrific outcomes for each of the boys involved.

So I kept tapping, kept up the mindless work that I could have done in my sleep because those scant hours were occupied with something else instead.

"I can give you access to the accounting package if you need something to make you utterly braindead," Marcus offered on my third evening with him.

I hadn't expected the wait to be so long; I'd thought the boys would have done their usual in-and-out style raid and for it all to be over within the first few hours. But now, that time dragged on, and I lost track of the hours I had stared at the screen.

I blinked. Realising Marcus was speaking to me — who else was there to talk to in the apartment? — and turned the words over in my head.

"Is this an effort to show me how many hours of overtime we both work?" I yawned widely, slapping my hand over my mouth. "I'm so sorry. My manners left with my ability to process life."

"It's fine," Marcus waved my apologies away. "But if you want more work to do, something truly mind-numbing, I can give you options."

"Gee, thanks for your generosity." I threw a puffy, gold pillow at him.

Marcus dodged it easily, grinning. "Careful. You'll muck up my hair."

I laughed at that, realising how quiet the apartment was.

"Marcus, you don't need to babysit me. Please, go socialise or whatever you do. Enjoy a night with a pretty girl. Or a man," I wiggled my eyebrows at him, expecting a laugh. But his gaze was dark and intense and far too similar to Liam's for comfort. "Stop that." My voice came out far too sharp, and I buried my head in my hands with a groan.

Every curl I owned and had a continual love/hate relationship with tumbled over my face. I left it all there, taking the moment of privacy I needed and Marcus, bless him, let me keep it.

A shadow cast light over my self-inflicted enclosure. I huffed at the strands and ended up staring down at Marcus' perfectly polished elf shoes. A secret smile warmed me from the inside.

Keep the memories close.

Liam's voice whispered in my mind, and I tugged the thought into me, stuffing it into the cracks that were already forming in my heart.

"Are you coming out today?" Marcus' voice held a note of amusement.

"You sound like King," I muttered, thinking of the young man who had replaced Cal. Liam might refuse to think of him that way, but the soldier even *looked* like Cal.

"Who?" Marcus' brow crinkled.

"Uh– just a friend of Liam's," I stuttered, mentally cursing the man who made me lie to one of my closest friends. I tossed up in my head if that was Logan or Liam for a moment too long. "Sorry. I'm really vague. I should go to bed." I snapped my laptop closed without shutting it down properly.

Marcus hadn't moved.

I looked at him suspiciously. Had I forgotten to eat? I checked my coffee, but both cups Liam had left for me were empty. I ignored the pang that thought created and focused on my housemate. "What?"

"You keep reminding me how empty my house is without anyone else in it. I actually missed you when you weren't here." Marcus brushed one of my curls from my shoulder with a crooked grin.

I stared, swallowing past the million thoughts that bombarded me.

You're not Liam.

And then I felt like a complete ass because I'd crushed the puppy-dog look on his face. "Have you just discovered the opposite sex?" I teased lightly, shifting back on the lounge, the plethora of soft cushions Marcus insisted on furnishing his house with crowding me. I gave one a push.

Marcus watched it topple off the sofa with a bemused look. "Maybe I have." He ran a hand over his head, shaking it out. The tousled ends fell in a haphazard mess that was so unlike Marcus but managed to erase twenty years of stress in an instant.

"Next, you'll be hitting on your roomie," I grinned, backing deeper into the pillows with an internal wince. Marcus watched me scoot back, still squatting in his elf shoes.

I bit back a laugh.

Now, who's inappropriate?

"Right? Who'd think it would happen?" Marcus matched my light tone,m but his eyes told a different story, a question rising in them that he knew I couldn't answer.

Are you asking me if I don't love him? If you can move in just because he's not here?

Am I going fucking insane?

My head screamed all the things at my business partner that I couldn't bring myself to say. Yet.

Marcus blinked; apparently, my thoughts were reflected in my face. Not that it was a bad thing right now.

"Rest. I need it. So I can tackle tomorrow head-on." My words came out disjointed as I made my escape.

Marcus rose, his hair flopping to one side. I laughed at him, the so out-of-character moment soothed by the image of the twenty-something boy that seemed to shine through.

"Is there any other way you tackle work? Or anything?" Marcus grinned ruefully, stepping back to give me room.

My mind flicked back to Jesse, kissing baby Aiden's head. And I made the decision actively then that whatever the outcome was for the boys — for *my* boy — I would stand beside him proudly.

Not that it wasn't a forgone conclusion, but for the first time, the words formed in my head.

I smiled. "Never," I proclaimed firmly, pleased it came out clear and loud. Tired feet dragged me to my room, though I heard Marcus in the kitchen for long after turning off my light. I stripped to a pair of boyshorts and exchanged my bra for a singlet. My fingers grazed the place on my lower back where Liam had touched me, the fading heat of him branded into my skin.

Keep the memories close.

I lay in bed expecting the restlessness, the grief to consume me as it always had, but for the first time in three nights, sleep came quickly.

Office days passed one after the other. Marcus drove me to the business in silence. It might have been uncomfortable on his part, but I spent time memorising every moment I had spent with Liam — how he had felt around me, inside me, the feel of his lips on my throat, the taste of his sweat on my tongue.

Marcus had largely left me alone after the night he'd made a pass at me, though the more I turned it over in my head, the less I was sure that he had made a pass at me.

Paperwork was delivered to my desk by an intern I didn't recognise. Still, I had been so invested in Logan's case for the past six months that I wasn't surprised the world moved on around me.

Now, I needed to make an effort to return to it.

"Thank you," I said softly, trawling through brain soup to find her name, "Cathy?"

The red-headed woman raised her eyebrows in surprise, and I wondered how many papers she had put in front of me and had no response from me before.

"You're welcome," she stuttered, backing away.

I smiled, not wanting to put her any more off-kilter, returning to my paperwork. The pen stalled in my hand. I lay it on the desk with care and flicked on my laptop. I had been as far out of the business as it was possible and *not* be actively involved. Marcus had offered to talk me through the accounts, and now that my caseload was caught up, maybe I needed to know what my business was doing with a whole lot more clarity.

"Cathy," I called as my intern had almost made her retreat.

She turned on her heel so fast, I thought she might give herself whiplash with her razor-edged bob.

"Yes?"

"Would you ask Marcus if he could talk me through the books? When he has time."

Cathy stared at me with her mouth hanging open for too long a moment. I nodded encouragingly and reached for a coffee cup. I raised it to my lips, but the damn thing was empty, and I winced.

"Of course. And...can I get you another?" Cathy gestured to my empty cup.

I smiled. "Please."

Maybe I could return to the swamp I had tumbled into without disturbing the peace in the office after all. My hand brushed over my phone, and I resisted turning it face up. Instead, I pushed it backwards, so it tumbled off the edge of the desk and landed into my overfilled handbag.

I needed to stop thinking about what Liam was doing every second of the day. The call would come when it did.

And if I held my breath, nothing would ever get done.

My double stack of coffee arrived in Marcus' hands.

"Peace offering? I've missed not talking to you." He pressed the mugs to the desktop. "But I understand. What I did was out of line."

"It's fine. You're going to regret that offer, though."

"Why is that?" Marcus hedged.

I grinned. "Because today, we're talking accounting."

Marcus groaned, flipping his phone in his hand. "Let me free up my day."

He regaled me with too many stories to recall, but the data stuck into my analytical brain, and I had made too many suggestions for improvements before the sun set over the city, my foot pressed against my handbag the entire time.

But no call ever came through.

CHAPTER EIGHTEEN

LIAM

The feel of her beneath me haunted too many waking hours and not enough sleeping ones. I would have disappeared gratefully into the memory of her, but it eluded me, leaving me torn between frustrated arousal and a desire to drop everything to claim her again.

But first, the inevitable.

"We're on." King hung up the call with a satisfied smile.

"Are you that eager to jump back into it?" I murmured as he gave me verbal directions to wherever we would find Logan nested up all cozy.

I fully intended to make *cozy* synonymous with *cold, empty cell.*

"Never far from it." King brought me back to the conversation.

Concentrate, you bastard. Distractions get everyone else killed.

I didn't like the reminder, but in this case, I wasn't unhappy that it kicked in. I wished I had taken the risk to see Cal before facing off with Logan and his groupies. King had filled his spot far too easily, but I missed the man who I knew would have my back.

On the other hand, if none of us walked out of today, then maybe Cal was in the best place and care he could be in.

The coward in me rose up on its toes.

I don't want to be the one to tell Mila Cal isn't coming back.

Though I suspected that would never have to be me. Black would claim that honour, and as Cal's ex-partner and Mila's carer, I didn't doubt he had every right.

"Get your head out of your ass and into the game, McNamara," King said softly, systematically checking his ammo.

I sent him an amused grin. "You know you'll get us arrested for having shit like that in the open."

"You want to get there, find they know we're coming, and not have everything in working order? Good fucking luck with that."

"Do you know something I don't?"

Something you want to tell me?

And there it was, in a single thought: the mindfuck that only Wayde Logan could deliver.

"After the clusterfuck of last time? Your smarts are in your ass if you aren't prepared for it again."

I grinned. The kid really was good value, and once this was over, I would miss the snarky side of him.

When it was over.

I focused on the road, refusing to think through the ramifications. The bottom line was that it had to be done, and it was my damn responsibility.

"Everyone in place?" We began to circle around the city in a familiar pattern, and my stomach sank.

"Man, if you wanted to ask the questions, next time, you take the call."

"You make it sound like it came from God," I joked, indicating before King could respond.

He raised an eyebrow. "The way that boy thinks, he might as well be."

"Awww, Mr Grumpy come out to play?"

I stared at the desecrated ruble that had been Micah's house. "I'm not doing this here. None of them will be able to focus."

"You calling it?" King asked from his place riding shotgun.

I stared at the blackened heaps of soot and debris, pipes and jagged metal striking up at all angles, all swept off the remaining footpaths and wrapped in a neat bow of police tape.

Any building near here would remind the boys how close Logan had been and how much we had missed him by. Just letting our guard down for a few hours, thinking it was all done.

The usual rush of pink sand was replaced by the warmth of Micah's loft, filled with the people I loved most. The banter, Selena pelting a pillow across the room, me stealing her garlic bread.

Cal's tired face, laughing and groaning at Mandy's messages before the dream was reduced to ash in my mouth.

"Yeah." I continued past the scaps of more than one life, already rusting at the tips. "I'm calling it."

The call to walk away was a popular decision. The call for radio silence until I got my head back on straight wasn't.

But like a troop of soldiers who trusted the orders they were given, they agreed.

Only King looked at me with a speculative glint in his eye.

We'd given up the suite I'd shared with Selena and returned to the small, double room we had shared from the beginning.

I rolled water around my mouth, rinsing away the salt that clung to my tongue post-workout, waiting, but the room remained silent. "Go on. Out with it." I swallowed, then tipped the dregs over my head, the cool water bringing the regular thump in my head down.

We were five days into an operation that should have been over within the initial forty-eight hours. Selena would be going spare, with no one to update her, and my body ached without the comfort of her next to me.

Without her near me regularly for the first time in years was emotionally taking its toll on me. Her ability to draw the hardest moments out of me, to nut through a problem when I let it fluster me, to bring me back from the desert...

Those moments displayed how strong she was, and the unfortunate bottom line was that I missed her like hell.

"We've been through this." King kept at his sit-ups, his arms crossed over his chest. "It needed to be done and finished. You let that slip away from you."

"It wasn't the right place. Everyone would have been out of focus. There were too many memories, too many chances that he would pull the rug out from under us. It is what he's famous for."

"You let a little thing like a downed building bother you? This is going to go all sorts of sideways." King shook his head, twisting to one side to stretch.

"It was more than a building." I pushed the words out through gritted teeth.

"Yeah? Because there was no man left there, Liam. You're letting ghosts rule your reality. Who's leading this fight? You, or him?"

King sat up, having barely broken a sweat, but I took his point.

"We're still following his lead." I bit the words off. "Fuck, I can't see beyond my own decisions."

"Fine. So talk me through it. And go see your boy in the hospital. But not the girl. You get all soppy and soft after you've had a good fuck."

I winced at his crass wording. "There's that gentleman's touch."

"Only if the situation calls for it." King grinned, accepting the water bottle I passed him. "Seriously, man. Go see your boy. No regrets, and all. I'll find you another location, and we will get your man there."

I nodded and headed for the shower without another word.

King might be twenty years or more my junior, but the kid had some serious smarts. I hoped he got a chance to use them in his military career.

A nurse smiled politely at me on her way around the ward. I returned it, sliding my hand into my pocket.

Being out in the open after hiding away for the best part of three weeks was crippling. I might as well have donned a red scarf and waited for the bull to come barrelling down the hallway at me.

But only another nurse and a handful of visitors passed me on my way to Cal's room, and too soon, I had my hand on his door.

I stared at my hand, willing it to have some sort of purpose of its own. King's voice made it past my somewhat fragile ego.

We'll get your man there.

I could have walked away and still known the job would get done. King might be one of a kind in his unit, but he fit well enough in ours.

Except that there shouldn't have been a place to fill, and only thanks to Logan, there was.

I turned the handle and entered Cal's room.

Machines beeped in a quiet symphony, their regular rhythm Cal's only companion.

I grabbed a corner chair, its utilitarian design perfect for my purpose. Swinging it around, I straddled it close to Cal's bed and slipped my hand around his.

The cold fingers lay lifeless on my own. Without the machines chattering at me, I might never have known he was alive.

"It's been too long, man. The shit we've had to deal with," I swept my hand over my hair, the buzz cut biting into

178

my palm, "I've missed your face like hell. But first things. I hear your girl is doing just fine. Fat and round and pissy as hell. Black and Jenny are having a bitch of a time keeping her in line. Ashley has coated Black's world in a sheen of glitter, so he's joined the pissy brigade," I grinned.

Cal would enjoy Black's submission to his girls as much as I did.

"I'm surprised that Jenny has managed to keep them all in line. That woman's a saint. The boys are doing well. Danny's performing exactly as we've expected, and Micah may be the best backup partner I've ever seen in that office. The two of them together — hell, if we can organise a new task force with them at the head of it, they will be unstoppable."

I looked for a hand shift, for anything; the thought of Danny doing well should be the thing that moved Cal the most, but he lay still.

I sighed and restructured my thoughts.

They aren't weighed down by all the baggage and shit that we have going on. Ally's stepped her game up. She won't stay. I reckon she'll head off and do her own thing, and we're just a stepping stone for her. Which is fine — her career was as fucked as they come, and if she can play ball with you boys, then she'll survive just fine on her own. She might even pick up a promotion at the end of this. And Brett's backed her." I skirted around the issue long enough to give myself a headache. "Selena. Ah, here's the biggest pit of worms I've cracked open." I leaned my head on the metal pipe that made up the back of the chair, its cold pressure easing the matching set inside my head.

Do I, don't I? You'd bitch slap me. We finally got together. And I love her. Yeah, I know," I grinned and banged my forehead gently on the metal chair back, " why didn't I do something earlier? Why did I wait if I'm just going to fuck with her, then leave her? It's a prison cell, or it's a box. There are only two possible outcomes for this. And I get the feeling it might be kinder for her if it's the box."

I waited for the slap across the back of my head that only Cal could have delivered, actually looking up when my skin stayed intact. "Hell, man. I come here to bitch at you, and you don't slap me down? You need to take lessons from Danny."

The memory rocked me. "Shit, what was that, six years ago? Seven? And all with Mandy fucking us all over. Tell me they told you about her. He cut her up and left her. Poor woman. Fucked up, and loyalties in the wrong place, but she didn't deserve that." Silence was my only answer. "Okay, fine, maybe she did, especially for this. Ha– now, I haven't replaced you but...we have a new friend. Son of one of my original guys, and a total ass. Reminds me of someone I knew a damn long time ago, who had blond dreads and could barely pull his first assignment together. Then fucked up the paperwork so bad I was digging you out of that Great fucking Dane ditch you put yourself in for three damn months. Killed me..."

I talked until my throat was raw. A few nurses stopped to look curiously at me, and one fed me, but for the most part, they left me alone. And that spoke volumes for Cal's state.

Finally, full dark settled over the hospital through the slim window that allowed a few bars of light into his room.

I rose, put the chair back exactly where it had been before and leaned over Cal's inert body to kiss the small amount of skin visible above his eye.

"Love you, man. Let's get this thing done, and then you're walking out of here with me."

For the first time in hours, I released the hand that had grown warm gripped in mine. I walked away from the man I considered my brother and prayed he hadn't heard the lie in my voice.

CHAPTER NINETEEN

SELENA

As it turned out, accounting put me to sleep far more effectively than anything else. Each night, I crawled into bed, mentally exhausted. Which worked out fine, most of the time.

Marcus managed to get over our disagreement. For several nights, I heard his door's custom squeak alert me to a visitor in the early hours and threw my earbuds in. It had been a long time since I had fallen asleep to music, but I picked out some of Liam's old, nineties grunge bands he'd convinced me to listen to back in uni.

The melody paired with the memory was a lullaby in itself, and I never heard the person leave, but no additional female was ever present at breakfast.

Marcus was far more buoyant, though I didn't rib him about it; our tentative peace had to hold while I lived in his apartment.

And still, no call or message came through.

"Do you need anything else?" Marcus popped his head around my open door, knocking at the same time.

I shook my head, gathering my things for my evening sojourn to the window. Late office evenings became all-nighters, and soon after, I developed a habit of sleeping there. My handful of belongings — seeing as I wasn't permitted to visit my townhouse without the boys, thus endangering them, Mila plus baby, Ashley and Jenny; could a girl have any more guilt shoved down her throat? — sat in a rotating bag that Marcus washed for me. His bachelor habits appeared far less than glamorous. However, I suspected he did it out of regret that he had essentially made me uncomfortable in his home, where I was supposed to be safe.

"I'm fine," I said when there was no sound of him moving away.

Glass thumped onto my desk, followed by a clink. I stared at the open bottle of red wine, blinking slowly.

"Sleep, Selena." Concern etched the corners of Marcus' eyes, the sprinkle of grey in his dark locks. "He isn't—" Marcus' mouth shut with a snap.

"He's not coming back? He's dead? He'll spend life in prison, and I'm wasting mine fretting after him?" I blinked clear eyes, staring back at my business partner. "I'm sorry if it came out rude, but I'll make my own choices."

I spun about in my chair, facing the floor-to-ceiling window that overlooked the city. My screen slid out of focus as I propped my feet on the pot of a large indoor plant. It was supposed to be healthy, though since it was still alive in my presence, I couldn't help but wonder if it might not be plastic.

My back stayed to the doorway until footsteps signalled Marcus' retreat. Some part of me might have felt guilty if it hadn't been that the man I loved was putting his entire career, everything he stood for, out on a platter for a psychopath. If I didn't stand next to him, with him, when it mattered, what was the point of it all? I refused to tarnish the few precious memories we had made together.

Usually, I curled up on the small, two-seater sofa typically reserved for clients when I was finished for the night when the screen refused to come into focus again. Otherwise, I spent the night staring at the empty doorway, wondering when Liam's bulk would fill it.

When that became an unfulfilled wish, I turned my attention back to my work, letting the city illuminate my new caseload. A poor replacement for Liam, but he was obsessive enough that he was likely stalking me from afar.

Some part of me perversely appreciated the idea.

After Trisha and Jesse's case, I hadn't touched family law again. It was far too close to my own situation, and the guilt and pressure lay on me heavily enough. Instead, I focussed on defence cases, honing my skills and researching as many benchmarks that might give me insight into how best to frame Liam's case.

I refused to believe he wasn't coming back to me.

One glass of the wine Marcus had thoughtfully provided told me how little I had been taking care of myself. Placing the crystal on my desk with an unsteady hand, I closed my laptop and stared at the lights of the city with unfocused eyes.

And slowly, I let the city drop away, replaced by memories of Liam. Fantasies of him walking through my office door and kissing me filled me. Some of the needier ones involved him hiking up my skirt and fucking me on my desk, but those ended in an unsatisfying orgasm, my fingers stroking over my clit beneath my skirt a poor mimicry for the real thing.

Those nights, I curled in my chair and stared blankly out at the city, wishing he could see me, the princess in the tower, waiting for the handsome prince to come and save me, to take us to a safe place where we could live without fear of Logan or retribution.

I couldn't breathe.

Just that single glass of wine was responsible, I was sure; that moment when a noise had woken me, and I suspected it had been my own snoring. Then cloth clung to my tongue, and I knew I was wrong.

Every inhale was met with a thick stuffing that closed over my open mouth.

I shifted, but nothing worked the way it was supposed to. My hands didn't separate, only jerking up and down like a marionette on a tangled string. My world was black and hot. Bile rose in my throat as my own breath hit me in the face. Lack of fresh air had always bothered me, and now I struggled to get it.

I blinked, licking at my mouth, but the world remained dark. I shifted again, tapping about with my feet.

Fingers clamped around my head. I jerked it away, only to connect with a very hard, very solid floor. Light filled my darkness for a too-bright moment, stars shooting across closed eyes, but when my sight cleared, the darkness remained.

My world was reduced to the inside of a black bag that muffled sounds as well as light. The throbbing in my head weighed me down. I sucked in a deep breath by reflex and choked on a mouthful of cloth.

Damp material stuck to my face as I shivered. Cold air assailed my skin. Was I naked? No. I still had pants. The thought made me laugh until the hands touched me again; bile mingled with a scream in an unfortunate gargle.

Someone had taken my jacket.

That same someone who was speaking beside me, trailing light fingers along my arm the way Liam always did.

Liam.

But this touch was different. Too soft, and something about it not so gentle, a threat held in reserve. Liam had an intensity about him that I would feel even if I couldn't see him or didn't know he was there.

This soft touch felt more...violent.

Voices chattered softly beside me, and I pushed at the static of panic that filled my head. One of the voices I knew, identified, would have known anywhere. Had listened to it a thousand times on recording, trying to work out an angle — any angle — to get the maximum sentence I could for the psychotic bastard.

Logan.

My stomach did a flip flop.

This was the man who blew up Liam's team, who almost killed most of us at least once, whether directly or through the bizarre style of mindfuck that he was infamous for. The boys had discussed it enough that I was overly familiar with Logan's life.

And somehow, I wasn't in my office. Or he was in it. My world reduced to a saggy black sphere around my head; I had no idea where I was.

Somehow, that panicked me more than anything else.

My stomach curled in on itself, a tight ball of panic that crippled me. I screamed my fear, but all that came out was a muffled whine. A hand patted my head, and voices talked over me like I was an unruly child.

It was the second voice that stopped me.

Something about it was...very familiar, like the familiar touch down my arm.

The type of familiar that I knew would come back to me around two in the morning. Normally, something I'd laugh over and wake Liam at some ungodly hour.

Except that this was far from anything funny.

It didn't belong to one of the boys, nor anyone else I would ever expect to rescue me from the mess I was in. That final thought cemented the feeling that this wasn't something I could fix on my own. No amount of smarts, no amount of screaming would help me here.

Think, for fuck's sake, woman! You're smarter than this!

But trussed up and blinded, the reality was simple: I wasn't.

My stomach stopped knotting and flip-flopping and began to curdle instead. Tears burned the back of my throat, and I willed myself not to vomit the meagre food I'd had. Drowning in a sea of my own puke was not how I would go out.

Logan might take that honour — I wasn't stupid enough to think my second run-in with him would end up rainbows and roses — but I wouldn't help him along the way.

The hand returned to my arm, tracing over my scar that ran from shoulder to wrist, the puckered skin a memento from the last time I had any sort of contact with Wayde Logan.

Sensation stopped. I blinked inside my bag, breathing shallowly, the scent of bile and stale red wine assailing my nose in the enclosed space.

The enclosed space that shrank as the bag was pulled tighter across my face. I tried to raise my bound wrists, but they were held down, too.

Before I could thrash against the restrictions, the material relaxed. I sucked in a deep breath as a hand closed around my throat.

In an instant, I was back in my townhouse, a different face leering above me but still a messenger of Logan. And in that instant, I began to pray to a god I hadn't spoken to since Liam's last flashback.

The hand on my throat back in my townhouse had relaxed when the cutting began.

But this time, it didn't relax, and the darkness inside my bag deepened.

CHAPTER TWENTY

LIAM

"Are you sure, this time?" King's question grated on me.

Too many hours wasted, too many days staring at Selena through a pair of binos while she sat alone at night, working. The second night I'd taken to watching her, she stopped working, staring at the empty doorway as though she expected someone to walk through it.

I swallowed roughly past the lump that blocked my throat.

She shifted in her chair, and I thought she would leave for the night. But from my side angle, watching her through my scope, I tracked her fingers as she drew her skirt up her thigh, her fingers disappearing between her legs. Her gaze never left that doorway as her skin flushed, her hips undulating in time with the way her wrist moved.

Heat washed over me, watching her touch herself, hardening as she bit her lip, pressing hard against herself. I imagined the cry torn from her, stifled as she came, but instead, I had to watch in silence.

Her hair tumbled forward over her face, her shoulders rising and falling in a ragged rhythm. When she raised her head, tears coated her face. She brushed them away with shaking hands, straightening her skirt. Slowly her breaths evened, and she turned away from the empty doorway, swivelling around, and I could have sworn she looked right through me.

My heart pounded against my chest cavity as though I were the one who had jerked off, but with King watching the door at my back, I had no chance for privacy.

I studied Selena, the slight flush across her cheeks the only evidence of her indulgence, but the sated look I'd memorised with her beneath me was absent.

But the lines on her face that hadn't been there before told me just how much the bullshit circumstances weighed on her, how much they weighed on all of us.

Her peace was just another casualty in a silent war.

"Ask me once more, and you'll find out," I snarled, not bothering to apologise.

"Deja Vu pissing you off?" King grinned.

I clenched my fist. Bitch slapping the kid would likely only result in a skirmish I didn't have the energy for — that and the fact I suspected King would lay me out on my tired ass.

It had dragged on too long. The surveillance, the waiting. More of the nothing that had filled our lives, wasting days that became weeks over the years Logan had haunted us.

And now, hunting him again, we'd broken our stride.

Until today.

"Location confirmed?" King slipped back into his *all-business* persona, and I envied his ability to cast off the mantle of patience that had worn so thin over my own shoulders.

"Yeah, we got eyes," Danny's voice crackled in my own ear as King passed me a transparent earbud. "Visual inside the building?"

Micah jerked his head, focussed on the screen before him, the drones giving him several angles of the initial industrial estate we'd identified. "Working on it."

A *friend* with a suspiciously military bearing and a very non-regulation haircut had waltzed in with a care package that included every piece of tech we needed. The flamboyant Asian man answered only to *Queen* and swapped his way around the room, picking holes in our strategy.

The sour looks on several faces would have made a nobleman's house proud, but it showed just how behind we were. Danny watched the soldier complete his circuit, and I had the pleasure to observe the moment he went into undercover mode.

The light, joking persona slipped over him better than any method actor in a long-running role. Moments later, he had Queen spilling every secret he could tell — and some he probably shouldn't have.

"It would have been handy to have this earlier, you know," I grinned to take the edge off my grumble.

"I thought this would all be over in a few days, you know. You dragged it out, Chief." King shrugged, but his lips pressed into a thin line.

"It's okay to fuck up in the field. It doesn't run perfectly every time," I said in a quiet voice.

King looked at me askance and said nothing.

"Doesn't fucking run perfectly anytime, you pair of assholes. Let's get this done. Mila's due in two days, and if I don't have this girl in a hospital then and knows she's safe, I'll be on a fucking rampage."

King turned his attention on Black. "Shit, man. I didn't know you had enough words for that."

I held in laughter that bubbled inside me. Black glared at the no-longer-so-newcomer, his fingers twitching.

"Boss," Micah's steady voice cracked, and every head in the room turned to look at him. Even Queen quit talking. "I– shit. Come here."

Black checked over his shoulder at the screen and froze.

Two strides took me to Micah's side, and I stared at the small group of people on the screen surrounding a lump on the ground.

"Is this the best you have?" I asked, staring at a group of legs from the waist down. Logan was easiest to identify; the baby blue suit would only be pulled off by one man.

Micah zoomed up to a higher window, zooming in to a pixelated screen that cleared in a moment. Two dark-haired men stood with their backs to us, and another two goons flanked Logan and his brother.

Joey stood with a side profile visible but still easily identifiable. Each one of them was chatting with an easy demeanour like they did this every day.

They probably do.

"Floor," I whispered, unable to force the words out.

Micah nodded silently, fiddling with controls until a clear view of several sets of shoes in various states of disrepair came into a grain semblance of focus. The lump on the ground included a pair of blue jeans and heels that could have belonged to any woman with a bag tied around her head. But there was no mistaking those chestnut curls I'd had a completely unreasonable love affair with for the better part of twenty years.

A harsh sound filled my ears, and it took until my throat hurt for me to realise the snarl came from me.

"We've got this," a soft voice came from my right. "I'll draw the assholes out. You get the other one."

"There will be two of them left. Plus her." I glanced down at Micah on my left, but he just stared at the screen, white-faced. King stood on my right, his hands shoved into his pockets.

"I'll kill him," I said in a raspy voice. It hadn't been in my head that I wouldn't try to bring the criminal in, but now, that option was off the table. I looked up at Black. "Tell me I'm only walking into this. If one of your girls is in there, I can't protect everyone."

That I wouldn't walk out again didn't cross my mind. But Selena would. I'd fucking well make sure she did.

Black smashed out a quick text and nodded. "They're clear."

"Fine." I grabbed the vest King had allocated to me, slipped a sidearm into the holster, and strode to the door.

"You're not going alone." Danny stepped in front of me.

"If you don't move, I'll put your sorry ass on the ground. Not one of you follows me. Is that clear?" I held Danny's uncertain stare as I waited for assent from everyone in the room.

Danny finally moved aside, and I was in the stairwell before I heard Queen's parting words.

"Well, for fuck's sake, why aren't we putting out the champagne?"

The short walk to my personal death row gave me the sort of peace I had only ever attributed to the calm before the war. Those moments between identifying a threat and calling action might be when another man might have his world flash before his eyes. For me, it was filled with the sort of silence that let me settle into my purpose.

I could have skirted the building, could have tried to line up a shot through a window, but Logan had already ousted me on that front. The thought that I might not be able to task the shot when it counted sat heavily with me. I accepted the failure, studied it, and discarded it.

Apparently, all I needed was a damsel in distress, and my midlife incontinent trigger finger was solved.

But she was *my* fucking damsel in distress.

And I'd damn well be the decrepit dragon that saved her.

I put my hand on the door and pushed it open.

When I walked into the warehouse, there were only three people inside it.

"You really are the show pony, aren't you?" Logan flicked his finger over the safety of his handgun.

I shook my head at him. "This isn't the time to play Russian roulette."

"Isn't it?" He aimed the weapon at his feet, and mine was up before he could flick his finger.

And I fucking hesitated. *Again.*

"Put it down."

"You've forgotten how to be a soldier, Liam. Shoot first, my friend."

"I'm not your friend."

"But you still want to play *cops and robbers*," Logan continued, ignoring me.

"You're a shitty actor. Put it down and step back. You too," I added to Joey, but my inside man didn't move.

He didn't smile, and any final advantage I thought I had left the warehouse.

My attention split between the two men; I knew I couldn't take both at once. My heart ramped it up a little, spreading adrenaline through my system at speed, as it had been conditioned to do, while the rest of me went numb.

The only question remained. If I killed Logan, would Joey kill Selena? What advantage could I give her?

Joey answered the question for me, aiming a kick at Selena's ribs that cracked. A faint whimper came from within her cloth-covered head. Selena wasn't a stranger to broken ribs, but I'd be damned if she would have to suffer more for my mistakes. Bringing the boys into the warehouse meant jail time or worse for every one of them, and I couldn't let that happen a second time.

"For every one of those breaks, it's an eternity in hell with me, you fucking prick." I let my anger unspool into my words.

Logan's cold outer shell cracked as he sneered at me, but his brother had the grace to look unsettled.

Good.

The smallest reaction was an advantage, and I would take everyone that I could.

The only advantage I missed right now was Cal at my back.

My rage released a little more, narrowing my vision to a pinpoint.

Joey looked straight at me and delivered a kick to Selena that shifted her body across the filthy cement floor, her cry audible.

I never took my eyes off Logan.

Pull the trigger, you ugly bastard.

My head yelled the words at myself, but I shoved them down. My hands were firm, but the perfect prince charming in me still wanted to write this off as a bad day in the office and live a happily ever after.

You know that's not how this will work.

I knew it, but I kept hoping for it.

"Don't kill the poor girl before I get the chance." Logan punched his brother in the stomach in a swift move, his weapon still aimed at Selena.

I stared at him while Joey wheezed. While that gun was trained on her, I couldn't risk the shot.

Joey's hand tightened on his gun, and he raised it, taking my hopes with him. But when he aimed it at Selena, that hope burned to acid in my chest.

Logan kicked his brother's ankle. Joey shot him a hard glance and lifted Selena, still not looking me in the face.

"Afraid of what you might see if you face the man you should be a coward for?" I grated, taking that acid and throwing pettily at the very small man before me.

"Did you think you had leverage over my kin, Liam?" Logan tsked at me as he wound his fingers around Selena's throat.

Joey planted his elbows on his knees, wheezing. Red flecked the cement Selena had lain on a moment earlier.

Logan tugged the cloth from Selena's head with his free hand, and it was back around her throat in an instant.

His gun never left the back of her head, the metal a dark shadow between her curls.

What do you want, you bastard?

Just fucking shoot him.

Cal's voice joined mine in a silent battle that raged inside my head. The ultimate distraction; fighting with your own ego and calling it something else.

Logan's mouth tilted up at the corner, Selena's curls obscuring the subtle rage on his face.

Selena stared at me, her face flushed in patches of pink and red. Her makeup was smudged, and all I wanted was to hold her and promise her the world.

But when her eyes met mine, the fear dulled to be replaced by a blazing resilience. There would be no begging there.

Just the staid, strong response I'd expect from her.

Fuck, I love her.

But this had to end. Here.

Logan pressed the muzzle of the gun against Selena's temple. She pressed her lips together, but I recognised the sound she muffled.

What are you doing—

Logan smiled again. Victory surrounded him.

He could win here. He had no one left. Unless he knew something I didn't.

Finally, it hit me.

I didn't blink. I didn't give him the satisfaction of knowing that after this, after all the years of chasing the asshole who tried to ruin my team, to know I'd recognised his suicide run.

He's *almost* ruined them.

But every single one had stood strong against him, not letting him in.

I could do no less.

I mirrored his smile with one side of my mouth. I knew it made me look psychotic; my last warrant officer had said so, right before his chest was blown open.

Then I wasn't so kind with my smiles.

Selena stilled. Even Logan seemed to sense the oncoming storm.

"If you wanted to be on Death Row, you could have asked. All that show, all the prancing...you're nothing more than a coward waiting for someone else to pull the trigger, so you don't have to do the time." My lip curled as I stared at him, but the barb missed its mark. I drew on my reserve instead. "Your daughter already knows you're psychotic. Shall I tell her how much her father longed for an exit that he set himself up to die? Pathetic," I spat, relieved to see the flicker of rage in those dead eyes.

If King truly wanted to see *soulless*, it was the man before me.

"My daughter gave up on me. She has no part in this." Logan shrugged indifferently as though taking the information and compartmentalising it away. The rage left his face.

My stomach curled on itself, my mind briefly flickering to the story Selena had told me of her client doing time who spent a blessed hour with his child.

Priorities and perspective.

"I did wonder why you didn't go after her," I said softly, letting my own fury hit boiling point.

Logan shrugged. "You've chased me for too long, McNamara. A little case of projectile impotence?" he laughed at his own joke, his fingers drawing tight around Selena's neck.

Her skin darkened the way it had beneath my touch, but for an entirely different reason.

For the first time, I recalled the gun I held, the trigger beneath the pad of my finger. By some miracle, my hands didn't tremble with exertion, my system flooded with adrenaline, the high still running its course.

"I made the shot before."

Selena with blood running down her arm beneath the hold of another man. I'd pulled the trigger with no hesitation then. Had saved her. The imminent threat. Why not now?

This was Wayde Logan. We'd chased him for almost ten damned years. He was a stain on our lives and so many others.

Would I be a stain on his?

The sidearm weighed little in my cupped palms. My sights fixed where I needed them to be.

"You won't be a stain on my soul," I whispered.

When he laughed, I pulled the trigger.

And hoped to God I'd aimed true.

CHAPTER TWENTY-ONE

LIAM

Nothing happened.

Logan's laugh bounced around my head, the only sound in the large, open space. Two gunshots rang out from outside the building, their distant retorts echoing through my body. He jerked, and I reciprocated, my hands strangely numb, waiting for the gunshot that would finally change everything in a far more permanent manner than I had been able to. The disabled gun sat useless in my hand for anything other than as a bludgeoning weapon.

But finally, my head recognised the double-tap from an outside source, the thump from above and beside me as something hit the ground.

The cool sensation of blood on an open wound, running down my hand.

The bastard had sniper backup to take the gun out of his hand, but why hadn't he taken the shot until now?

I let the half-grin remain on my face, closing my fist. "I brought my own."

"Of course you did." Logan sighed with the air of long-running patience. He shoved at Selena's back with an expression of extreme disdain, as though all this was beneath him.

You're the one who set this up, you bastard.

My mind ticked over; how close had King been to take that shot? And how fast would local police arrive in a deserted area on a Saturday morning?

Selena stumbled several steps forward, coming to a rigid halt in no man's land, caught between Logan, Joey, and me.

"Did you think I would leave anything up to chance when it came down to your little vendetta, soldier?" Logan's smile split his face in an obscenely white grin. "Nothing is a chance. Everything is calculated."

He nodded to a side door of the large room I hadn't noted when I entered the space, too focused on the collar of red beads that dotted Selena's throat.

Marcus stepped out of the shadow behind him, his face as cold and dead as Logan's.

How the fuck have I missed all of this? How long—

I closed my eyes for a brief second. The betrayal rocked me, then the descending failure.

I can't save her any more than I could save them.

Pink dust coated the inside of my eyelids in dry grains that scratched every surface, though it had been a long time since I had last experienced it in person. But the nightmares had kept me current.

I opened my eyes to stare straight at Selena, panic widening her own as they darted to one side then back to me. Her bound hands clasped over her stomach a moment before she retched coffee on the filthy cement floor.

"I'm sorry, Liam," Joey said the words softly, and to my surprise, they came out sincere.

I frowned. "It's a shitty position to be in, Joey. But you have a choice now." Addressing Marcus was out of the question.

Selena's business partner and friend stared at Logan with glazed eyes.

We had all seen that sort of obsessive devotion, the sort Logan was famous for encouraging in small-time crooks. It looked like he had been recently stretching the mark.

Or maybe it hadn't been so recently at all.

My mind began to accept the circumstances, began to work it through. However, I also accepted I had made it to the party way too late to change anything unplanned at this point.

Logan laughed again, and I knew that if I lived through this, that sound would fuck with my sleep for a decade to come.

"There's no choice, is there," Logan's words fell flat, making it a statement, not a question.

"I knew he was with you. Since the warehouse. Who the fuck uses their baby brother as bait?" I eyed Joey, praying he had actually flipped to me, but as I caught Selena's wild-eyed gaze, I got the feeling this was one screw-up we weren't walking out of.

"The sort who doesn't take traitors well." Logan's voice held an edge of steel.

I recalled the raw lines crisscrossing Joey's stomach, the mess his side had become and wondered at Logan's motivational methods. How he managed to keep these obsessive people on his side when they turned from ours so readily.

I had trusted too many people, and now my poor judgement would cost more than just my life.

The sick sensation that moved the floor beneath my feet stilled at another sound.

Footsteps filled the warehouse. Footsteps I knew well now and didn't have to look to know who was behind me.

Black, Micah, Danny.

King.

I allowed a dead smile to creep across my face.

"No. That option is off the table now." I rose, reaching back and taking the fresh weapon King slipped into my non-master hand, his own arm extended. Dark metal glinted dully in the filtered light.

Joey gripped his gun tight, his arm jerking. Selena's eyes weren't the only wide ones as Logan took in the crowd at my back that slowly filed into the room to circle around the brothers and the traitor.

"Put it down, Logan," I offered again, though the mad gleam that lit his eyes from some dark place deep inside him told me how wasted those words were.

I held the handgun in a gentle grip, raising it just to the left of Selena, who stood in the centre of all the hardware, her eyes flicking from one face to the next.

Marcus swivelled from side to side like a bad film extra and totally useless. Eventually, he settled his aim in my direction, and that suited me just fine.

A movement to my right turned my head a fraction, but to my shock — and, it seemed to everyone else's too — Joey's gun was trained on Logan.

His brother sneered, what could have been an elegant expression of disdain, had it not been for the soulless eyes that stared back at his kin.

"Look at me, sweetheart. Just here," I said softly, with a smile that excluded everyone else in the room, "and Selena?" She nodded, her lips parting slightly, but nothing came out. "Don't move."

Shots rang out, and four bodies fell.

CHAPTER TWENTY-TWO

LIAM

Chestnut curls tumbled over my wrists as I dug them deep beneath Selena, cradling her to my chest. "Sweetheart," I rasped, sweeping hair from her porcelain skin, her eyes closed and face so peaceful.

Danny yelled something from my side, his hands pressing over a wound that ripped into her shoulder. Her blood mingled with mine, tears dripping from my face to wash away the stain on her skin, only for it to be renewed a moment later.

Hands tugged at me, and I ignored them all until Micah's large face took up my vision. Without speaking, he very gently slid his enormous hands beneath mine, pressing over the wounds on her back.

"I love you," I whispered, my mind already replaying the moment every trigger in the room was pulled with Selena at its epicentre.

Her eyes stayed closed.

Paramedics removed her from our grip, tending to everything required with cold efficiency.

I sat in a puddle of blood, surrounded by bodies, but this time, some of it was mine.

Sirens rang out around us, covering the industrial estate in a flood of lurid light unsuited to a Saturday morning. I sat beside Selena, still unmoving on her stretcher, my unbandaged hand wrapped tight around hers.

Three other stretchers were laid out, but the bodies needed to fill them weren't in any hurry to get to their final destination.

Micah and Danny bickered with King, who had taken a shot through the bicep, a clean straight through he refused to have seen to, apart from a basic stuffing-and-bandage job. He shook his head, sending me a quick grin before he disappeared around one of the ambulances.

Black had done his own vanishing act, heading back to his girls and to get Mila to the hospital as soon as she needed to go.

Which meant we would be taking up three rooms.

I sent a prayer up in thanks, tagging a desperate plea I couldn't voice with every thought.

Micah leaned into the door, cleaning his hands with a bunch of wipes that did little to fix the mess. I stared at the blood, gripping Selena's white hand tight.

"She'll be okay. We'll see you there, somewhere between her and Cal's room," the big man called as the paramedic jumped into the back of the ambulance, calling instructions. The vehicle began to move, and he closed the doors belatedly but not soon enough to hide the fear that crossed Micah's face.

I answered the paramedic's question by rote, staring at her, and let the rest of the world fend for itself.

Two hours later, I sat leaning against the wall outside Selena's room. She was only a few doors up from Cal, so if anything changed for either of them, I could run in either direction.

The convenience of tragedy.

Mila had made it to the hospital, too, though not for any reason other than to sit with Cal. Weeks had passed since she had last seen him, since the girls had been hidden, and Black had done a fine job of it.

So now, all we had to do was wait.

My ass had gone numb long ago, shaping itself to the hospital floor. After a while, the boys left, my unending silence too much for them, and wandered down the hall where Black and Jenny waited. Ashley had already begun to redecorate the wing with glitter.

And I waited for the shakes to set in.

Everyone had taken their shot, and we had gotten off lightly, with only the wound to King, who brushed it off as an everyday hazard. Joey and Marcus had dropped, though I had no idea who had taken the shots, which I had told the local police time and time again. My shot had been saved for the man who threatened the woman I intended to spend the rest of my days with.

Due to the nature of the scene and the single shot each of us fired, we hadn't been arrested, which surprised me to no end. That was until Micah leaned down and whispered that Danny had filed the general situation as an undercover case the moment we'd discovered Logan was free.

For that, the young cop was due a promotion.

There would still be legal tape, but with three weapons aimed at a civilian, the use of deadly force was permitted, providing it wasn't excessive, and fortunately, we had all covered our asses on that one.

Finally, Selena's doctor approached me. I rose on unsteady legs. The man opened his mouth to speak, but I cut him off.

"Start with the bad and work backwards."

The doctor looked at me with hard eyes, but whatever he saw there softened him. "That shoulder already has significant nerve damage. Had she told you how much?"

I nodded jerkily. Hell, I'd been there when the damage had been inflicted upon her, and now a second time. "Yes."

The doctor surveyed me for a long moment, exhaling in a short puff. "Selena won't have a lot of movement there. Potentially ever. She'll need extensive rehabilitation, and she has a broken collarbone. She'll struggle for months, and only if it heals well will she not require further surgery. In some cases, we can remove scar tissue that causes ongoing chronic pain, but—"

"You're telling me she'll live," I grated out the words, not having spoken for several hours.

The doctor stared at me. "No one has spoken to you?"

I shook my head. "No."

"My God. Yes, she'll live, and while there will be pain and some aesthetic damage—" he stressed the word, but I waved it away.

"As long as she heals, that's what matters."

"We can do that, son." The doctor smiled at me, his stuffy face lighting with relief I suspected mirrored my own. "She's barely awake, and she will need to sleep. Ten minutes."

I nodded, a block in my throat barring access to my voice.

He left the door open, and for the second time, I witnessed one of the people who mattered the most in my life hooked up to more machines than should be required to live.

Selena turned her head so slowly, her dozy eyes bloodshot. "Liam." Her voice was a thread of a whisper, lost amongst the bleeps.

"Sweetheart, I haven't left you. And I'll stay. I'm never leaving you again." I kissed her forehead, stroking over her cheek with my fingers. Blood caked into her hair where it hadn't been cleaned off properly. As soon as she could be moved, I promised myself I'd make sure the nurses helped her.

Selena stared at me, the hint of a smile teasing the edges of her lips, but whatever drugs they had her on were too strong, and her focus slipped, her eyelids closing softly.

I gripped her hand tight, selfishly needing to draw her back to me. Clenching my teeth, I hooked my foot around the leg of the single chair in her room, dragging it to me without letting go of her. And be damned what the doctor wanted, I held her other hand, kneeling beside her bed.

I got to keep her. That made her sound like a puppy, or maybe that was me, but I wasn't arrested, I wouldn't serve time, and I wasn't dead. My gaze flicked over the bandages covering her shoulder. White scar tissue from her previous encounter peeked out the top, surrounded by a field of pinkened, swollen skin.

My girl and I hadn't been able to keep her safe — a second time. But still, she was my girl, and I would work every day to earn her love and forgiveness for not being there at that right moment.

Selena sighed in her sleep, her head falling to one side. Her lips tightened, her eyes crinkling, and my heart clenched, skipping a beat until I choked. She made a little whimper. I stroked my hand over her face until the lines of pain smoothed, and to my everlasting shock, the tears began to fall.

Selena slept, and despite the doctor's words, they let me stay with her. An hour after that, a yell from along the corridor shifted me. I strained on stiff muscles, the events of the past three weeks hitting me now that I had my girl back. I eased my way between the bed and the chair as Danny threw open the door.

"Shh!" I hissed, glaring at him.

The young cop's face split in a broad grin. "C'mon! You need this," he ushered me out of Selena's room, sprinting up the hall to Cal's.

Nurses yelled from within the room, their frantic shouts echoing down the corridor. Black appeared out of the doorway but barged his way back in. I reached the same spot, a step behind Danny, and peered into the chaos beyond.

Some part of me was reminded of the first night we all arrived at the hospital after the bombing, and my stomach rose. I fought back the bile that tinged my throat with acid and a metal taste, but not a single nurse had that false edge of happiness we had experienced then.

Every one of them panicked, and every one of them hovered over Mila.

Cal's wife was surrounded by a puddle of pink fluid, arching on the floor, as much as a full-term pregnant woman could. She leaned forward on her knees, gripping the arm that Black held out to her, the deep indents in his skin a gauge of her pain.

Danny and I hung back, peering into the room.

Nurses cleaned frantically as they tried to move Mila, but neither she nor Black appeared inclined to move. He knelt in front of her, talking quietly, neither of them acknowledging the flurry of activity around them. The doorways were just too small. By the time a gurney arrived to transport Mila to the birthing suite and the commotion that followed in moving a woman in labour, it was too late. Baby Hugo Dane was born by necessity, right next to his father. Finally, the nurses seemed to accept the situation. They helped Mila out, cleaning around her while she held the tiny human. Black directed everything from the doorway where they tried to shoo him away, but neither Mila nor Black would have it.

Hugo went on the breast just as Mila's stretcher made it into the room, with mum and bub placed unceremoniously onto it and wheeled out the door.

The ruckus filled the corridor, but from my spot diagonally opposite the door, trying to peek without being a nuisance, I saw the movement, and suddenly only one voice filled the corridor.

Every face turned to me, but I just pointed into the room, my hand finally shaking.

"Show me my son," Cal rasped, his whisper faint, his eyes barely peeled open, and yet we all heard it, lulled into silence by the pair of miracles we bore witness to.

I remained outside the room, having taken my brief greeting with him, even if I doubted Cal could see me. Mila clutched Hugo as she crouched by his bed, supported by a nurse on one side who tried to look insignificant, with Black on her other side. He said nothing, from what little I could see, still at my post between the rooms of the two people I loved most.

But in her few minutes before unconsciousness reclaimed Cal, I watched him touch his son's face, love blazing from his as I witnessed the tear that tracked over the tubes and bandages that covered his face.

And for a long moment, he even locked eyes with me.

Mine were damp when I wandered back into Selena's room. The nurses had enough on their hands other than me, so I perched next to Selena's bed in a clinical, overstuffed armchair, lacing my fingers through hers, and closed my eyes.

CHAPTER TWENTY-THREE

SELENA

A pair of matching, giant coffee cups rested on each arm of Liam's favourite armchair, my name emblazoned up the side of one.

Between Liam's hand and my damaged shoulder — the same one as before — we were a great pair, cuddled up together in a space we both admitted that it would be a stretch to get out of without harming either of us.

"Please tell me one of those is for me," I eyed the coffees as sunlight streamed through the broad glass back of the house that overlooked the city, "And you're being sneaky," I added.

Liam had dragged my sleepy backside out of bed, my brain still drug-addled, and my shoulder sore from yesterday's physio session, with the temptation of coffee that I still hadn't gotten to touch.

"I wanted to enjoy the morning with you." He raised an eyebrow. "Is that so bad?"

"I was enjoying the morning in your big, warm bed." I batted my eyelashes, but his expression didn't change, so I thwacked him lightly with my good hand instead.

"Ow?" he asked mildly, running his hand through my hair. The bandages had come off with no issues, other than a jagged scar that ran from his thumb across to his wrist. Liam never complained, and he never had an issue with it.

I wished I could say the same for my shoulder.

"Can I have my coffee now that you've personalised it?" I nodded at it but slid my arms beneath his shirt, needing to touch his skin. "Mmm. You're warm."

"Thanks to you. I should never have—" he broke off, a haunted look in his eyes.

"You didn't put me in danger. Logan did. Remember?" I stared up at him, loathe to move my head from his chest where his heart pounded against my cheek. I leaned up to kiss the stubble on his jaw, anyway. It was the first time since uni that I had seen him with any at all.

It wasn't the only thing that had changed. Liam hadn't mentioned Logan by name, making him the nameless demon of the house. And just to prove my point, I used it as much as possible.

Liam tilted his head down, his grey eyes catching and holding mine. A thrill raced through me at their intensity. "I remember you on the floor with a bag over your head. I remember thinking that I couldn't save, not even by throwing myself over you," he ground the words out, catching my mouth in a searing kiss that sent tingles to my toes.

I shifted against him, my eyes still half-closed. "How can you be so dark and intense and make me horny at the same time?"

Liam laughed — a deep rumble that grew in his chest and moved upward. He reached around me, gathering me closer in one arm. "I love you so damn much. But you got hurt on my watch, so I wanted to make up for it."

I frowned up at him. "How are you going to make up for that? Wait, you don't *need* to make up for anything– oh." My personalised coffee mug arrived in my hands. I cradled it carefully. "Why is my name painted down the side?"

"So they know who to call for when you drop in your cups," he smiled, "and I'm conscious of your habit of so many takeaway cups and that clashes with my recycling beliefs. So." He shrugged with a good-natured grin, his eyes dancing merrily.

"So?" I narrowed my eyes. "Since when have you ever been a *so* man? What are you up to, Liam McNamara?" I turned the mug cautiously in my hands, inhaling the ambrosia within. My name was followed by another, but it wasn't Liam's. Or, more precisely, it wasn't his first name. "What—"

"Don't choke," Liam murmured in my ear, his lips brushing the sensitive spot at the curve of my neck.

"Don't choke?" I'd become a parrot, repeating everything he said. "Why would I—" The first sparkle caught my eye, my brain catching up as I read his last name after mine. The ring was balanced against the lip of the coffee mug, and the diamond winked as merrily as Liam's slate grey gaze.

"Marry this old grunt who can offer you nothing more than the protection of his body. And maybe a big, warm bed," he added.

I swallowed, my gaze sliding between the ring and his face. My mouth dried, and I was suddenly aware of how loud his heart pounded against his chest.

So you can really hear a heartbeat outside someone's body when they're nervous.

Apart from snarky observations, my brain had left the building.

"Selena..." Liam prompted me softly, though his gentle tone didn't disguise the growing edge of desperation in his voice.

"Oh." My brain ticked over. "Yes. Yes! A million times yes!!"

I pressed harder against him, attempting to kiss him and juggle my precious coffee at the same time.

"One of these things isn't working." Liam detangled himself, switching out my coffee for the ring and sliding it onto my finger while I mewled pathetically after my coffee. His fingers slid beneath my chin, tipping my face back to kiss me deeply, filling my entire body with warmth.

"Yes. I'll marry you," I grinned and found my joy reflected in his face. "Now, can I have my coffee?"

Liam shook his head, a bemused smile curving his lips. "Only you, Selena."

CHAPTER TWENTY-FOUR

LIAM

The wharf beside my father's seafood shop was covered with a small crowd dressed in their Sunday best. My father still fit into the suit he had married my mother in and refused outright when I tried to update his wardrobe.

Cal, Mila and Hugo clustered together, both the picture of love and because Cal was still unsteady on the prosthetic that had replaced the mangled flesh Logan had stolen. But as I looked around at the group of my closest friends who were more family than anything else, I realised Logan gave us far more than he had taken.

Selena's hand rested in mine. I closed my hand around hers, the engraved, two-toned wedding ring on her finger the perfect match to my own. My chest swelled as the celebrant closed off the ceremony, and I was glad I didn't have to speak again because, for the life of me, I knew I wouldn't be able to.

Her fingers shifted in mine, and I blinked to find her staring at me expectantly.

"Your turn," she murmured softly, but her eyes blazed with suppressed laughter and joy.

Someone laughed in the background, and I could have sworn it was Danny.

I slipped my scarred hand through her curls, studded with tiny pearls, like a mermaid princess come to land for her sojourn, drawing her into me.

When my lips touched hers, the rest of the world dropped away for me. I sank into the softness of her skin, her hands trembling against my chest. The salt mingled between our lips, and I couldn't tell whose tears they were.

"I love you," she smiled, her face glowing with radiance.

I murmured the words back, barely able to get them out when they jammed in my throat, but she seemed happy with my stunted gurgle. My hand slipped around the small of her back to hold her to me while we were announced to the crowd, which erupted.

Cal grinned from ear to ear at me, hobbling his way forward alone to embrace me and the tears followed faster for both of us.

"Congratulations," he said gruffly into my shoulder.

I held on tight, not ready to let go. "You're more a brother to me than anyone," I said quietly, and Cal's grin got bigger. He dipped his head toward mine.

"Hey, no kissing my man!" Selena protested to a myriad of giggles from Laura and Jimmy, who had swamped her.

Cal laughed, leaning forward. "Then you're about to become a godfather twice over again."

"You're having twins?" I stared at Mila, then back to Cal. "How– when—"

Cal shrugged easily. "Let's just say everything works to full capacity."

I clapped his shoulder, my smile creating my face past aching point, but I didn't care. "Congratulations, you lucky bastard."

"Isn't he?" Danny nudged his way into my hug. "Cuddle?"

I groaned and heard a grumble nearby that could only have come from Black. Ashley darted around, tossing a liberal volume of unicorn glitter over everyone while my father passed champagne around. I hadn't been able to talk him out of serving people food or Micah's mother out of cooking.

In fact, my father and Micha's mother appeared to have hit it off.

Danny chattered in my ear as Micah wrapped his huge arms around us all. Congratulations echoed off the jetty. I laughed, finally able to release every strand of knotted, unmanageable panic and anger, releasing it all.

The laughter died back, general chatter resuming. Laura tugged at Selena's dress from all angles, Mila passing baby Hugo across to the stunning bride.

Mine.

Selena tossed me a look of abject panic as she took the tiny human, and Mila whispered her news in Selena's ear.

I shook my head, wondering what it might be like to have tiny feet running about my house.

"You're taking my job, of course," I broke into the conversation surrounding me to address Cal, who stared at me with wide eyes.

"What? Hell no; I can't—"

"You've done a fine job, more than could be asked of any man," I cut him off.

Cal's eyes narrowed. "Then what are you going to do?"

I looked for Black, who stared at me with hard eyes. After a moment, he lifted his chin in a half nod. "Him and me? We're retiring."

"We've earned it," Black grunted, wrapping his arms around Jenny and Ashley. "And we're next because that's the only way I can adopt this little unicorn."

Jenny burrowed her red face into Black's shoulder while Ashley entwined herself around his waist.

"Which means I need help." I looked for Danny and Micah, catching both their attention. Micah straightened, and Danny looked alarmed. "You two. Pick a team, and don't fuck them up. You'll get orders on Monday. From him," I jerked my chin at Cal, who resembled a fish out of water. And having dropped that bomb, I clapped the boys once more on the back and nonchalantly went to find my mermaid.

Selena broke away from the conversation to slide her arms beneath my jacket, linking her hands behind my back. The long scar started at a hand's breadth of mangled flesh at her shoulder, joining with her first scar that ran to her wrist. Her strapless dress hid none of it, and she told me time and again that she was only proud of them because it meant we had all survived.

I loved this woman more than anything. Anyone.

Swallowing hard, I kissed her with as much reserve as possible. She made it difficult, pressing her body against me in all the right ways.

"Damn, you know everything about me, don't you?" I curved my hand around her jaw, cradling her in a gentle hold.

Selena just giggled, leaning her cheek against my chest with a contented sigh.

I pressed my chin to the top of her head, looking out over my family. The girls danced around the jetty while the boys were already nutting out new jobs. Micah's mother and my father flirted, and every one of us was covered in glitter.

Movement caught my eye from the end of the jetty where it met the land. A lone figure stood there, dressed in jeans and a white tee. I squinted, but I didn't really need to. King was easily recognisable at a distance. He gave me a slow nod.

I held his gaze, trying to detangle my hands from Selena's hair without dislodging half the pearls woven into her glossy chestnut locks. By the time I had managed to extract one to motion King to join us, the wharf was empty.

The parking lot that surrounded my father's shop was as vacant as before, and there was no trace of the young soldier who had earned his place in our broken family, who had stood beside me when I'd needed it the most.

Cal passed me a flute of champagne, offering a toast that ended in cheers that ran the length of the jetty.

I held Selena to me, memorising every member of the team who had banded together as brothers for so long. My family.

Selena tapped my arm, bringing me back, a quizzical look on her face. "Are you okay?"

"I'm fine," I kissed the end of her nose, and she swatted at me, tugging me to where my father had helped lay out tables. As we congregated around the aromatic food Micah's mother had provided, I couldn't help but give one last glance to look for the unsung soldier who had done so much and disappeared without so much as a thank you.

ABOUT THE AUTHOR

Sofia Aves writes fast-paced police romances, suspenseful mysteries, steamy cowboys with a Montana backdrop, and the occasional cheeky god. She loves reading Indie authors and hides her collection of college romance books beneath an ever-growing TBR pile.

Sofia is a mum of three crazies and an overly large fur baby who thinks she's a teacup puppy. She loves orchids but can't always keep them alive. Sofia lives near Brisbane, Australia.

www.sofiaves.com

Join Sofia's newsletter & get a free Blue Blooded Brothers short story:

https://BookHip.com/CNMQFX

Follow Sofia on BookBub:

https://www.bookbub.com/profile/sofia-aves?follw=true

Did you like Noah King? Read the first chapter of KING, Z Boys book 1 here...

PROLOGUE

I wasn't always a clean-shaven sharpshooter. In fact, growing up as an Army Brat to a special forces Dad, I was a royal pain in the ass to everyone I interacted with. Hours spent with spray paint cans at the back of the fields on the base while Dad was working where I wasn't supposed to be in the first place. Entertaining myself with discarded ordnance shells and making keyrings for imaginary mates from used ammo.

My childhood.

It was about as far removed from *normal* as anything could possibly be. No mother, because she had left shortly after Dad returned from the desert with a shiny, albeit destructive, new aspect of PTSD. Deployments weren't conducive to having a family, though I watched other kids play with two parents with ill-disguised envy.

Those imaginary mates from every army base around the country became real mates as I grew into my teenage years, junior officers and younger troops wanting to show off their knowledge to someone who understood.

229

Because I *did* understand.

I lived the life with them, the few weeks of the year the unit spent at home; watched them train, read their tech and procedural manuals.

Until I became one of them.

CHAPTER ONE

KING

My mark wore a pink and black chequered tie that clashed horribly with his date's dress. She, at least, exuded class. Even from the top of the residential block opposite the high-end restaurant, I could see that.

My hands gripped at empty air, missing the familiar shape of my rifle, but I was under strict orders to leave it at home.

I could have as easily parted with my legs.

"Nothing." Scotty '*Joker*' Evans rocked back onto his heels, jiggling about. Ever struggling with the serious side of our work, we could always rely on a smart ass comment from him amid gunfire. Hence, his callsign.

We had all earned them, in one form or another.

"Sit still, you old bastard," I groused. "Don't they teach you anything useful in the RAF?"

"Piss off, King. You might actually learn something if you shut up once in a while." His British accent thickening, Joker gave me his trademark grin, one that many a lady —

both young and not so young — had dropped their knickers for.

I snorted softly, turning my attention back to the politician and his date. After his pedicure, he had met her at his regular restaurant, not far from the expensive suite someone else rented for him.

The man wasn't influential yet, but he had the potential, which put him squarely on our radar.

Find out everything you can about him and file it for that rainy day when you'll need to use it.

Anything to protect the nation, even if it was several oceans away and twenty years in advance.

Joker continued to grumble beside me.

The politician — I winced again at his truly horrendous taste in ties — rose, tossing his napkin to the floor with disdain.

I zoomed in on my helmet display, studying her face and then his. Had he hit her up for the night, and she had said no? He had definitely misread that one.

His date folded her arms, looking away from him as a herd of waiters congregated about them. Even from the top of the next building, their fussing was overly pronounced.

I wondered if they were as keen to get Ugly Tie out of the restaurant as his date clearly intended.

A woman at the table behind turned to study the commotion, and I nearly dropped my kit.

Stunner.

Heavy lashes and dark, wavy chestnut hair were distinctly out of place in an exclusive restaurant in Cambodia. I shook my head, mentally tracing over her toned figure tucked into something red and sparkly.

Not the time or the place, King.

My mark moved the fastest he had in weeks, and naturally, I wasn't even watching him. He stormed through the restaurant's doors that were held open for him, the doormen bowing low. He sank into a car waiting at the curb, although his rented residence was only a three-block walk.

I tapped the radio at my side.

"Ugly Tie incoming. Same as usual." I smirked; it wasn't the first time my mark had left a date, though it *was* the first time she had kicked *him* out. I suspected it was his not-so-sweet talking skills. Or maybe he had terrible bedroom eyes.

"...the fuck? Reception's shit. Bald Eagle? ...moving?"

I snuffled a laugh. "Yeah. That one. See you back at the block."

"Don't go changing designators over the radio, man." Lucas Kelly — *Hearts* — berated me in a whiny tone as soon as I stepped through the door of the holiday unit. The small section of Z-Unit cramped into a space that should have held four teenagers on schoolies at the absolute most.

Instead, three highly-trained military operatives hand-picked from their careers were stuffed into it, though technically, none of us existed on paper anymore.

Wires and parts of computers lay in a haphazard mess strewn across the entire combined lounge and living area, surrounding the oversized mass of muscle planted in the centre.

"Fuck, it's like walking into Beruit." I stepped gingerly over some cords I thought weren't as critical and trod on some that were. Hearts moved, and I flinched. "Seriously. Can't we look at these people before we name them? Ugly Tie is so much better than Bald fucking Eagle."

"It's not like we're naming *us* or anything that matters." Joker laid our surveillance kit on the table in a clatter of tech that hadn't been packed up properly.

"Damn, man." My flinch became a wince. "Will Mr Politician be replaced by the next gung-ho politician when he runs out of cash or sponsors? Yes. Will he run out of dates due to social ineptness? Also yes. Don't you ever feel sorry for these bastards?" I retraced my steps and claimed the bags of tech before Joker could damage anything further.

"You want me to feel sorry for a rich prick who bleeds poor people dry so he can live his rich prick lifestyle?" Hearts glared at me over his shoulder, pointing back the way I had come. "Plug that one back in. Talk about pricks," he muttered, tapping away frantically.

"How long do we keep tailing Ugly Tie?" Joker asked softly, running a hand through his hair.

I grinned. "I knew it would catch on."

"Seriously. The worst thing these local people do is poach from wildlife reserves because they're starving." Joker stuffed his hands into his pockets. "That's not a crime."

"Hell. You are in a mood."

"We've been here too long."

"You're both a pair of whiny bitches. We're out in three days. Two more on recon, then we catch our flight home." Hearts shook his head, the behemoth of a man leaning forward, reading data from four screens at once.

"Home, man." Joker cheers-ed me with his water bottle.

I downed mine and headed for the bedrooms.

"Where are you going?" Scotty called after me.

"I need to run."

Ignoring grumbles from the other two, I retreated into my spartan room and tugged off my protective vest, stripping back to bare skin. The kevlar didn't weigh that much — and every one of us had trained hundreds of hours wearing it — that it felt more naked without it than in it.

Every muscle had tightened with too many hours of surveillance. The inactivity killed me in more ways than one, but at least I wasn't as fidgety as Joker. I trotted down the fire escape stairs, jumping the last few steps to hit the ground running.

Twenty blocks later, I turned around. Those same tight muscles burning, I sprinted for as long as I could hold it before dropping back to a jog. The run wasn't just to keep my body going; the muscle that needed the most work was my brain.

Being cramped into a hotel room for nearly three months with only basic surveillance work had come close to crippling me. My two hours out each night might eat into my allocated sleep time, but my brain — and my body — were grateful for it.

Every inch of my body burned by the time I hit the fire escape for the return journey, my lungs sucking at air that wouldn't fill them as I sprinted the final flight.

The rest of my unit was already down by the time I crept back into the room.

Two days never seemed so long. Ugly Tie did his usual rounds both mornings: collecting his coffee and blow job from the delivery girl he under-tipped for her tenacity and service under duress. Lunch was a simple affair involving lots of booze and too many associates who sat close together, so there was no room for anyone to stab them in the back.

Dinner and another failed date.

On the second night, Ugly Tie stayed in.

"That's unusual." Hearts was still tapping at his keyboards in the apartment. "Stay with him, make sure nothing changes. Don't blow this on our last night. I'm keen to be on home soil." He punctuated his last words with a harsh tap.

Both Joker and I winced at the spliced static assailing our ears.

"He'd better do nothing." I adjusted the settings on my visor, but it didn't give me any greater insight on my mark.

"He's made two calls, hasn't eaten, and now..." Joker trailed off, squinting as he repeated my process, "he's going to bed? The hussies have worn him out."

"We're done, then." I stretched my calf slowly; the thing had gone to sleep beneath me.

We packed up in silence from then until we hit the street, the local night markets still active. Joker checked his shoulder as he stepped out onto the street, jerking backward in a hurry as a tuk-tuk tore past him, a very retro beatbox pounding in his wake.

"Hell, you do need to go home." I laughed as he cursed.

"Yeah, well. Home isn't home, is it?" he snapped cryptically, his cultured British accent thickening with his irritation. Finding a break in the traffic, he jogged across the road, leaving me on the other side.

The months we spent out of the country cost us plenty, but even so, none of us really had the lives others might expect. A regular special ops soldier might not be permitted to talk about his work, but to the rest of the world, Z Boys just didn't exist.

Heading home did sound good, but Joker was right; we were headed for Australian soil. His home was halfway across the globe.

I inhaled my last few hours of Cambodia, relishing the lights and never-ceasing buzz of the place.

"Any chance you two can actually keep up?" Heart grunted as we headed for a small and inconsequential airfield.

Situated a few blocks from our hotel, it gave us a chance to hop onto a local charter and onto another, smaller plane to eventually land on military soil for our flight home.

Customs saw soldiers ready to head home, manifests provided from our cover unit dated months ago. The pilots saw a pretty piece of paper with our false records, which they ignored.

"You make it sound like you're struggling, old man." I grinned at the big man's back, knowing he'd probably kick my ass the next time we trained together.

Which would probably be the day after we touched down on home ground.

Hearts had a good decade on me in skills and training, but my determination to push all his buttons equalled that.

"Just keep moving." Joker loped by me, his long strides eating mine.

"Taking the order to *blend in* a little much, aren't you?"

The tall man's shoulders sloped, his back slightly bent, though his pack weighed little. Each of us had been in our civvies for so long, I knew it had begun to impact our mindset. Uniform was part of the training, part of the conditioning that kept us strong, focused.

I wondered if Joker even remembered how to march. Ace would kick our backsides into gear in a few days.

We left the monotonous drone of the main streets behind, pushing through the outskirts of the town. Joker disappeared into foliage ahead, the track marked by a well-trodden patch of mud that disappeared between two trees.

A shadow passed across it, then another.

I frowned; neither was big enough to be one of my boys. Jogging the last few steps, I sloshed through the mud, a new drone filling my ears from the front. But the shadows had disappeared across the foliage, not into the airfield beyond.

A handful of lean-to huts stood off to one side in a clearing, their occupants flitting about with menial, day-to-day tasks. A tiny figure darted into a hut, followed by a head of dark, chestnut waves.

My frown deepened. I glanced back to where Hearts and Joker had disappeared, but something drew me toward the lean-to.

Swearing softly, I slid the zip on my backpack, digging in to find my sidearm. I held it at my hip, fumbling with my other hand for the magazine.

The tiny hut was even tinier from the doorway. People scattered as I approached. Inside, a woman huddled on the dirt floor in a hunched ball, talking quickly but soothingly to the shadow of a child I had seen earlier.

A knot grew in my stomach as I realised they weren't alone. Money slipped from her hand to the child, who disappeared across the other side of the house and out through a window.

The woman turned to face the only other occupant: a man holding a matte black submachine gun aimed at her. He made a gesture with one hand, but she shook her head, clutching the strap of her laptop bag strung across her chest.

"*At louy,*" she said in a clear voice.

No money.

I blinked. Reacting calmly in a shitty situation didn't come naturally to most people. It was something trained into your brain as you weighed the options in front of you with a clear assessment of what the outcome of each action would be.

Standing in the shadow outside the man's line of sight, I loaded my weapon and took another look at her.

I need to know who you are.

The ability to do that probably came down to how I dealt with the threat before me. In a darkened space on the outskirts of town, this was only going to end one way, and for the woman, it just came down to how messy the outcome was.

"She doesn't have any money." I held my arm just slightly behind me, as though reaching out to comfort her, edging into the hut. "You saw her give it away."

Large eyes swung my way, but I gave every inch of my attention to the man demanding it.

"I don't want her money," the man's English was better than I expected.

"Good. You hop out of here, honey," I said softly, flicking my finger behind my back.

Those eyes widened in my peripheral vision. The moment she began to move, I knew it was a shithouse idea to try to remove her from the situation she had gotten herself into without creating a greater threat than I could offer.

"Stay. Please," the man's cordial words were disputed by the jiggling of his weapon. A second armed man appeared from the other side of the hut — from a rear door, I assumed, as he didn't use the window the child had. Probably *why* the child had used the window as her exit strategy. This day was just getting better and better.

I tried hard not to wince. "I need to take her home," I said firmly, sidestepping across the woman.

The tip of the gun followed my movement. Objective achieved.

More movement from the side of the hut I had entered from, but this time they were familiar shadows, which gave me additional options.

"She stays. Fun times," the man smiled.

I wished he hadn't. Several teeth were missing from it.

It was a moral choice on two fronts which may or may not have been altruistic. Save the girl, and fight the fight, because that was what we were trained for. And with his weapon aimed at me, I had a hall pass for what came next.

A simple aim and depress of the trigger.

And called that fateful word that would bring us all together.

I dropped to one knee.

"Contact."

KING releases May 13, 2022

Pre-order his story here

BLUE BLOODED BROTHERS

COLLISION

Book 1

Mila dreams of a pair of cold, hard eyes every night. Only five years past, Wayde Logan robbed the bank she worked in, killing her friend and co-worker. A hot-shot rookie cop let the criminal mastermind get away, but in the rush, Logan left his daughter at the scene. No longer the loose cannon that allowed Wayde Logan to escape, Callum Dane is a fast-tracked task force detective, hunting the only man who has ever escaped him.

Five years ago, Mila was held up in a bank heist. While she survived, her co-worker didn't. Nightmares of the criminal genius' cruel eyes have plagued her since his escape at the hands of a rookie, hot-shot cop.

Callum Dane is still chasing his nemesis. Wayde Logan is the only man he's failed to put behind bars, and who nearly destroyed his fast-tracked police career. Now, Cal is the leader of an elite, police task force dedicated to hunting the bank robber, but for five long years, Logan has evaded capture.

When he rear-ends a car while distracted by his frustrating ex, Cal and Mila are thrown headfirst into a maelstrom of events that brings them face to face with the man they both fear.

POLITICS & PAPERWORK

Novella

Liam is constantly swamped beneath the politics of managing an elite task force. Now, given more downtime than he can handle, the ex-special ops sniper flounders to find purpose outside the strict rigours of his working day.

Selena has been Liam's best friend for nearly fifteen years. Elegant and intelligent, and a partner in her own law firm, she's helped Liam through difficult cases, as well as the aftermath of PTSD. Watching Liam drown in day-to-day life, Selena ups the stakes with a little flirting to restore life to the man she adores.

When a series of vandalisms target Selena, Liam is determined to keep the captivating solicitor safe, so long as she lets him. Intent on playing her game by his own rules, Liam risks an uncertain future for the woman he's always loved.

BLINDSIDED

Book 2

As the youngest member of an elite task force team and built as big as they come, Danny is often underestimated. It's an image he encourages, despite sporting a genius level IQ. Currently screwing his boss' ex and with a big problem for authority, Danny is sent to professional development coaching. He hates the idea – he's got determination in spades to do what it takes in his job and personal life, and thrashes against it until he meets Laura, the sexy motivator who shows him he is worth more than what he believes. When the team begins working Operation Predator, Danny's moment of peace is shot to hell.

Danny is sent to professional coaching as part of his boss, Cal's, efforts to hold the team together after their last operation. When he discovers his motivator is the gorgeous jogger he's been working out with, Danny is determined to flirt his way through his coaching, stubbornly refusing to delve into personal truths he's been hiding from himself for years. He's relieved when he's placed on an undercover assignment – his preferred area of expertise.

Moving in with a group of gym junkies isn't a bad way to spend assignment – especially when he gets to hack as well. The group remove small change from banks, but Danny feels there is something bigger in the works – until he is spotted by Laura, who almost blows his cover. Pulled from his assignment, Danny is furious. Tensions rise during their coaching sessions as more odd hacks catch Danny's attention.

Their budding relationship is blown to pieces when he opts to go back undercover, determined not to let Laura distract him.

SENTINEL

Book 3

The man with a black heart has found someone to love.
Theodore 'Teddy' Black is the veteran of his ex-partner's task force.
An exceptional knife fighter and hand-to-hand combat expert, he's
perfectly placed to infiltrate an illegal cage fighting ring. He's also
head-over-heels for Jenny Smith, foster mum of criminal mastermind
Wayde Logan's daughter.
Jenny, the focus of his live-in protective detail.
Even though Logan has been denied bail, his reach extends further
than Black would like. Jenny and her foster daughter Ashley are
placed in safe house after safe house, the moves taking his protective
detail into the public eye. With both Jenny and Black living on a
constant knife edge, tension explodes between then, an attraction
neither can try to deny. Jenny knows better than to get between
Black and his job, but she manages to push the strict boundaries he's
set her. When he promises her a single dirty night together, she
doesn't know if it's the start of something incredible, or the end of
everything she cares about.
Black can't believe he's offered Jenny what they both crave. He
knows it's a bad idea, but he can't keep his hands off the woman he's
sharing the ghost of an existence with.
When the cage fighting assignment conflicts with his protective
detail, Black is strung between his loyalties.

IMPACT

Book 4

What does the ultimate adrenaline junkie do when the stakes get personal?
Always chasing his next high, Micah Riveria makes the biggest bang he can – whether it's a new explosive to play with, lifting the biggest weights he can, or pushing the limit on the competition monster truck circuit. While the task force winds down after a big win, Micah spends more time at the track working with Jimmy, the geeky computer girl with green hair who tweaks his truck to perfection before every comp. Some of the drivers are looking for bigger highs that the pro circuit can provide, and Micah is swept up in a game of ultimate stakes — with Jimmy at the centre of it all.
There's no job, no assignment, so the team take a break — and Micah heads to the track. He's content to talk geek with Jimmy, live odd hours and get away from the expectations of the team and family. In the midst of his r&r, he finds himself suddenly part of a group of adrenaline junkies, pushing themselves and their limits — further and further.
As their behaviours become more erratic and desperate, Micah discovers theft beneath it all — and people begin to get injured. He calls it in to Cal who tells him to stay in — perfectly placed to drive the investigation. As his relationship with Jimmy heats up, he realises she might be right at the epicentre.

RECKONING

Book 5

TRICKSTER'S LAW

A child isn't born evil...is he?
Mischiefmaker, silver tongue, trickster... Mayhem follows Loki throughout the nine realms, earning him a reputation as a bringer of chaos. But there is more to Loki than mortals see, and life is boring for an immortal when no one really gets him.
A little mischief is harmless in the hands of a god, right?
Companion to Odin and Thor but shunned by the Norse gods of the Æsir, Loki still seeks their acceptance. No matter how many times he saves their supreme backsides, his every effort ends with a death threat casually tossed in his direction.
Increasing his attempts to impress the Æsir, Loki tires of their constant disdain despite his successes in their impossible challenges.
So, he turns to what he does best: chaos.
Follow the trickster god Loki through the perfectly normal life of a disillusioned god, and find out what makes him NOT SO...EVIL.

SNOW ON THE RANGE

Red Hart Ranch

Every Christmas, Red Hart Ranch opens their doors, and Montana
provides the perfect backdrop for good company and better food.
But this year, the table won't be as full.
Eve Beaumont is a twin heir to Red Hart Ranch. She loves the land,
loves the people, and will do anything for them. Christmas sees most
of the ranch hands return to their own homes to celebrate. Only a
few long term cowboys remain with the family.
When Eve and her brother Trav go into town to collect supplies,
they each bring home a drifter for Christmas. Rhys Archer and
Simon Haldon are as different as two cowpokes can be. One rough
edged who can work the land and animals with a firm hand; the other
a smooth talker with a devilish charm. Eve finds both men attractive
against her better judgement, but when tragedy hits the ranch,
romance is the last thing on her mind.
Vandalisms happen around the ranch, and Eve isn't sure who she can
trust. She knows neither man is who he pretends to be — but when
no one listens to her, she has to prove her suspicions on her own.

www.ingramcontent.com/pod-product-compliance
Lightning Source LLC
Chambersburg PA
CBHW010553170726
48285CB00011B/2886